BRINGING EZRA BACK

CYNTHIA DeFELICE

BRINGING EZRA BACK

Orchard Hills School
Media Center

FARRAR STRAUS GIROUX • *NEW YORK*

Copyright © 2006 by Cynthia C. DeFelice
Distributed in Canada by Douglas & McIntyre Ltd.
Printed in the United States of America
Designed by Symon Chow
First edition, 2006
10   9   8   7   6   5   4   3   2   1

www.fsgkidsbooks.com

Library of Congress Cataloging-in-Publication Data
DeFelice, Cynthia C.
    Bringing Ezra back / Cynthia C. DeFelice.— 1st ed.
        p.   cm.
    Summary: In the mid-1800s, twelve-year-old Nathan journeys from his farm on
the Ohio frontier to Western Pennsylvania to rescue a friend held captive by the
owners of a freak show.
    ISBN-13: 978-0-374-39939-9
    ISBN-10: 0-374-39939-5
    [1. Voyages and travels—Fiction.   2. Frontier and pioneer life—Fiction.
3. Freak shows—Fiction.   4. Rescues—Fiction.]   I. Title.

PZ7.D3597 Br 2006
[Fic]—dc22

                                                        2005049763

To Buzz, again

BRINGING EZRA BACK

The state of Ohio, 1840 . . .

AN ITCHY FOOT means you'll soon go on a journey, folks say. If it's your right foot that itches, you'll start off for someplace far away. If your left foot is the itchy one, you'll go where you're not wanted. Mama had never set store by such notions, and I reckon she was right. But *both* my feet were itchy, and I couldn't help wondering what it meant.

I took off my shoes, got one look at the bumps and blisters, and had my answer. Like a fool, I must have stepped in the poison ivy vines that grew behind the barn.

I climbed up on the fence I'd been mending, and scratched my feet hard against the bottom rail. The rough wood felt good.

As long as I was taking a rest from work, I figured I might as well play a few licks on my fiddle. Since Pa got it for me, I took it with me wherever I went. When I was

teasing sounds out of it, I forgot most everything else—
including, I hoped, itchy feet.

I'd been playing for a while when a man appeared
before me real sudden-like, out of nowhere, or so it
seemed. Without thinking, I raised my right arm. I
wished I'd been honing a scythe, or sharpening Pa's
knife, or cleaning his rifle. At least that way I'd have a
weapon in my hand instead of a fiddle bow.

"Whoa there," I said warily. "Who are you? And what
do you want here?"

The man stopped and held up his hands, with the
palms open toward me. "Whoa, yourself, young fellow,"
he said. "There's no call to be so tetchy."

I reckon I *was* touchy. In the year past I'd met a man
called Weasel, and from him I'd learned there are people
whose hearts are blacker than a moonless night. I'd gotten lost in that darkness, so lost I couldn't see my way
out for a long time.

Since then I'd worked hard on the farm and had taken
up the fiddle. Both helped to keep my mind off Weasel.
Still, memories of him got mixed up in the jobs I did and
the tunes I played. I reckon a body can't lose the knowledge of something once he's got it.

For one thing, I couldn't take to new folks right off,
the way I used to. I didn't mean to be standoffish, but I
could never be sure about a stranger, whether he was
likely to want to do me harm, the way Weasel had. Pa
and my sister, Molly, were about the only people I
trusted. I'd say Mama, too, and our friend Ezra, but they

weren't with us anymore. Mama had caught fever and gone to the next world. As for Ezra, he'd gone west to find his wife's kinfolk, and Pa and Molly and I didn't know if he ever got there.

I told myself this feller looked harmless enough. He was wearing a pack like the one Isaac the Peddler wore when he stopped by our cabin each spring and fall. Molly and I looked forward to Isaac's visits more than just about anything else all year.

"You peddling?" I asked.

The man nodded, and smiled broadly.

"Isaac's always been the one to come out to these parts," I said.

"Isaac gave up the traveling way of life," the man informed me. "He got himself a little store back east. Said he was too old to be toting a pack around in the wilds with nothing but God's earth for a mattress and pillow."

Isaac had always said he meant to settle someday, but I never reckoned he'd actually do it.

"I wouldn't say no to setting this pack down and partaking of a bit of refreshment, if you take my meaning," the man said.

Mama would have asked me where my manners were, keeping a visitor standing in the barnyard after all the miles he'd traveled. "I reckon you'd better come on inside," I said.

The man tipped his hat to me and smiled again. "Orrin Beckwith, at your service," he answered, giving me a little bow.

"I'm Nathan Fowler," I said. Then I forced myself to add, "Welcome to you."

We started toward the cabin. I hollered to Molly and she poked her head out the door. When she spied the peddler, she disappeared for a moment, then came out to meet us with a cup of cider in her hand. Duffy and Winston raced beside her, barking with excitement.

Pa was busy splitting firewood at the far end of the pasture. I whistled, loud, to get his attention. He straightened up and peered in our direction, his hands shading his eyes. The sun was pretty low in the sky, which meant Pa would be coming in to supper soon. But no matter what time of day it was or what we were doing, we always left off working when the peddler arrived. Sure enough, as soon as Pa saw us standing next to a figure with a pack on his back, he took one last swing with the axe, put it up on his shoulder, and started toward us.

I introduced Molly to Orrin Beckwith. Shyly, she handed him the cup. He drained it in one long gulp and let out a loud belch. Molly's eyes widened, and she giggled behind her hand.

"Pardon, young lady," said Beckwith, belching again, only quieter this time. "But that was far too delectable to sip politely. Is it your own home brew?"

Molly nodded.

"My compliments," Beckwith said, with another little bow.

Molly giggled, and I could see how pleased she was.

"May I ask you a question?" Beckwith said to her, real serious-like.

Molly looked surprised, then nodded again.

"What kind of bushes does a rabbit set under when it's raining?"

Molly's face twisted up the way it did when she was thinking hard on something. I was pondering the question, too, and the man's reason for asking it. Finally, looking disappointed, Molly said, "I'm sorry, sir. I don't know."

Beckwith paused for what seemed like a long time before he said solemnly, "Wet ones."

Molly shrieked with delight. "A riddle!" she cried. "Ask another!"

"All right, then," Beckwith said with a sly grin. "Here's an easy one for you. I turn green into white, then into yellow. What am I?"

I was interested in spite of myself. I thought and thought about it, but I was certain I'd never heard of anything that could make colors change like that.

Molly stamped her foot and pretended to frown. "That's not an easy one!"

"Want me to make it easier?" Beckwith teased.

"Yes!" Molly answered.

"I eat green grass and give white milk, which gets churned into yellow butter." Beckwith raised his eyebrows and waited.

"A cow!" Molly said.

I groaned. It *was* easy, once you knew the answer. I should have guessed it. After all, ever since we'd got our cow, Golly, it was my job to milk her every day, and Molly's to make the butter.

"Ask another!" Molly begged.

"All right," said Beckwith, acting as though Molly was plain dragging the questions out of him, "if you insist. Ready?"

"Ready," said Molly eagerly.

"Many of them go to the spring, but they never take a drink. What are they?"

Pa had been approaching all the while that Beckwith was talking, and he was close enough to hear the last question. He bent over and whispered in Molly's ear. She grinned real big and said triumphantly, "Footprints, that's what!"

"Well said, Miss Molly," answered Beckwith. "And I can see your father is no fool, either."

"I don't know about that," said Pa, stepping up to shake Beckwith's hand. "But I wasn't born yesterday, and I've heard a few riddles in my time. Welcome to you."

We all headed for the cabin. Inside, Pa put his axe down, and Beckwith took off his pack. He set it carefully on the floor, then commenced to rub his neck and shoulders.

I noticed Molly was staring fixedly at the pack, and I knew what she was thinking. She could hardly wait for the moment when it was opened. Truth to tell, neither could I. Accustomed as we were to making or growing most everything we had, we plain treasured the sight of the city-made goods and fancy notions the peddler brought.

After hearing the news about Isaac, Pa said, "Did you stop off in town, Mr. Beckwith?"

Orrin Beckwith nodded. "Spent two nights and a day there. Bedded down in the livery stable and set out first thing this morning for you folks. Took me since sunup to get here."

It would be dark before long, so I wasn't surprised to hear Pa say, "We'd be pleased to have you stay for supper, and the night, too, if you'd care to."

I tried to push down the uneasiness that rose up inside me at the idea of a stranger stopping off with us. We'd always welcomed Isaac to spend the night. Anyone who came this far would expect the same.

"Thank you, sir, to both of those kind offers." Beckwith rubbed his hands together and looked around the cabin. "Something does smell mighty good," he said.

"It's stew," Molly said. "Nathan shot a squirrel yesterday, and I made blue biscuits."

I smiled. Molly was ten years old, and ever since Mama died, she'd done most all of the cooking chores. I reckon she didn't notice the look on Orrin Beckwith's face at the mention of blue biscuits. I'd felt the same way the first time I'd watched Ezra add ashes and maple syrup to his cornmeal dough. Beckwith would soon find out how good it turned out.

Beckwith waggled his eyebrows at Molly and said, "Speaking of blue, I have some indigo." He leaned down at the same time to take something from his pack. "It's come all the way from India."

"Indigo! Did you hear that, Pa?" Molly said excitedly. "Some blue in my quilt would sure look pretty."

"And I have madder root," Beckwith went on in a teasing sort of voice.

"Oh!" Molly gasped. "That makes red! Mama always said there's nothing cheers up a quilt like a touch of red."

"The good ladies of town agree with you there, Miss Molly," Beckwith said. "They'd have bought up all my dyes . . ."

I watched Molly's face crumple with disappointment.

Beckwith grinned at her. "But I said I needed to save some for a certain young girl I'd heard tell of who lived a mite farther on."

Molly's cheeks flushed and her eyes sparkled. It was good to see her so happy. I wasn't sure I favored the way Beckwith was going about his business, though. He was making out that he was doing her a special favor, when he was only trying to get her to buy his dyes.

"Oh, and one of those good ladies from town sends her greetings," Beckwith went on, with a sly wink in Pa's direction. "A certain Abigail Baldwin asked me to pass along her best wishes to you all."

It was Pa's cheeks that turned red then. Pa had danced a fair bit with Miss Abigail at the spring dance in town, and Molly was hoping she might be our new mama someday.

With another wink, Beckwith reached into the pack and held up a horn comb and some brightly colored hair ribbons. "You may be interested to know she was admiring these, and everyone present agreed they looked right fetching in her auburn hair."

Molly said, "Oh, Pa, they *would* look pretty on Miss Abigail, don't you think?"

I knew Molly could use help with her chores, and she said she wanted some female company to talk with, instead of just me and Pa all the time. So I didn't say what I was thinking, which was that I liked Miss Abigail all right, but I didn't much take to someone new being part of our family.

Pa answered Molly with a nod, and looked regretfully at the ribbons. He didn't make a move to take them, though, and I knew it was because we had little money to spare for fancy things.

Then Orrin Beckwith turned to me and said, "For you, young Nathan, I have the latest in straight razors from England."

I was twelve, and hadn't noticed even the first sign of a whisker.

"If you're not shaving already, you'll be needing to before my next visit, by the looks of you. Why, you're near as big and strong as your pa."

I was flattered at the notion that I looked grown

enough to sprout a beard like Pa's, but I didn't let on.

Beckwith eyed me close, sizing me up, it seemed like, the way Pa might look at a horse he was fixing to buy. "You hold your cards mighty close to the chest, don't you, son?" he observed. "Now that I think on it, I imagine a sensible young man like yourself is more interested in practical matters."

He took a knife from the pack. I knew right off it was a Barlow. My friend Colin Whitefield, whose pa owned the store in town, had one.

Orrin Beckwith held it out to me. "In my humble opinion, this little beauty is the single finest tool there is. A man out here on the frontier has to be prepared to protect himself and his family, and to do the work that needs to be done. For example, you were mending fence when I showed up."

I'd taken a break from fence-mending to play on my fiddle, as Orrin Beckwith well knew. He gave me a smile, like we shared a secret, and I scowled at him.

"This knife will notch out a fence post like cutting butter. You'll find it comes in handy for just about any chore that comes your way. Take it, see how it feels."

The blade was so shiny I could see my own face staring back at me. I felt the blade with my fingertip. Sharp. Strong. All of a sudden I wanted it, not as much as I'd wanted a fiddle, but nearly. I looked at Pa.

"It's a fine knife, Nathan," he said. "But I reckon for now we can make do with mine."

I felt a stab of disappointment, and looked away so's

Pa wouldn't see it in my face. I knew he'd had to trade a wheel of our homemade cheese, some dried beans, some animal pelts, and some money on top of that, to get me my fiddle. I couldn't expect to get a knife, too.

I handed it back to Orrin Beckwith without a word. But I felt like somehow he knew how much I wanted it. It unsettled me to think he could see right through my skin to the inside. I wished I could do that, instead of wondering all the time what folks might be thinking.

Then Orrin Beckwith said, "There must be something here I can tempt you folks with." With a flourish, he opened the pack all the way up. Molly ran over, squealing with excitement. She exclaimed over each and every splendid item Beckwith took out and spread on the table for us to see.

There were cards of buttons and papers of pins, hooks and eyes, spoons, bowls, plates, rings, brooches, washboards, liniments for horses and for people, too. There were shoelaces, silk and cotton goods, Bibles, and almanacs; handkerchiefs, candles, seeds, caps, gloves, and mittens. If I hadn't seen it all come out of that pack, I'd have bet money—if I had any—that it would never fit back in.

Molly was sniffing a cake of sweet-smelling soap, and running her fingers over a shawl Orrin Beckwith said came all the way from China. Suddenly Beckwith looked at Pa, who was working a pair of scissors in the air, getting a feel for them. Pa was squinting his eyes to get a better look.

Orrin Beckwith's expression grew almost crafty. "You a reading man, Mr. Fowler?"

"Yes," said Pa. "But now that you mention it, it's been getting harder and harder for me to make out the words."

I looked at Pa with interest, and some worry, too. "What do you mean, Pa?" I asked.

"Well, say you used your mama's quill and ink to write something, and then a drop of water fell onto the paper."

"The ink would spread out and make the letters all wiggly," I said.

"That's what letters look like to me these days," Pa explained. "I have trouble with what's right in front of my face, but I can see clear across the far pasture just fine." He gave a little shrug.

I tried to imagine what it was like to see all wiggly.

"Mr. Fowler," Orrin Beckwith said, breaking into a big grin, "if you'll step right over here, I believe I will be able to fit you with some spectacles that will solve this troublesome problem in the wink of an eye." He laughed at his little joke, then untied a cloth pouch and unrolled it. Inside were about ten pairs of carefully wrapped spectacles. "There are five different strengths," he explained.

I heard in his voice that he was proud to have such fine wares.

"It's a matter of finding the right strength as well as the proper fit. Please," he added, gesturing for Pa to help himself.

I watched as Pa put on one pair after another. Molly handed Pa one of the Bibles from the pack, and with each new pair he moved the book closer, then farther, then closer again. "Hmmm, that's better," he'd say, or, "These make my head spin!"

Finally he said, "Well, now, isn't that something?" He continued reading for a while. Then he took off the spectacles and said, "Mr. Beckwith, I thank you. Someday, when we've saved up a bit, I aim to get me some of those specs. In the meantime, I reckon I can see well enough."

The cabin was real quiet for a minute, except for the snapping of a log in the fire, and I figured Molly and I were both thinking the same thing. We wanted Pa to have those spectacles. But unless every corn plant had three ears come harvesttime, I didn't see how it was going to happen.

"We'll take some of that indigo and some madder root," Pa said. "And I expect that'll be it for this trip, Mr. Beckwith. I'm sorry you had the trouble of coming all the way out here for so paltry a sale."

"Oh, thank you, Pa!" Molly said.

As she gave Pa a hug, my eyes caught on a pile of handbills and broadsides that had fallen out of Beckwith's pack. Isaac had always carried such papers with him, too, so we could see the words to the latest songs, and read whatever news somebody had thought to print up. Orrin Beckwith said, "Go ahead. Have a look."

I paged through the stack of papers. The first ones were all songs. The titles made me laugh: "The Lawyer

Outwitted" and "The Old Maid's Last Prayer." Then there was one called "Confession" that wasn't music at all but the last words of a man who was about to be hanged for murder. I wondered who would want to read such a thing.

The next sheet looked interesting. At the top, in real big letters, it said:

☞ Not to be Missed!! ☜

Reading on, I saw it told about a traveling show.

See Human Oddities,
Curiosities,
and Monstrosities!

***

THE PRICE OF ADMISSION IS ONE DIME,

☞ TEN CENTS ONLY, ☜

MERELY THE TENTH PART OF A DOLLAR!

***

FEATURING CALVIN EDSON,
THE HUMAN SKELETON!

It said that this feller Edson was the world's skinniest man, which I thought might be something to see.

Next it told about Little Miss Mary, who was a

grown-up lady only two feet tall. I thought I might like to see her, too, as well as the Amazing Amelia. She was only nine years old and weighed over four hundred pounds, which I reckoned was quite a lot.

There was a person called Pea-Head Pete and another by the name of Bearded Betty. But before I could read more about them, I saw something farther down the page that made me cry out in horror.

Pa, Molly, and Orrin Beckwith all turned to me. "What is it, son?" Pa asked quietly.

I didn't want to say the words I'd seen. It was like speaking them out loud would make them true. Wordlessly I put the paper on the table and pointed.

☞ SEE THE WHITE INJUN,

A MAN WITH NO NAME AND NO TONGUE! DEAF AND DUMB,

FROM WHENCE DID HE COME? SAVAGE OR CIVILIZED FOLK? WOMEN, CHILDREN, AND THOSE WITH FAINT HEARTS, BE WARNED...

"It's Ezra," I said into the terrible silence. "Who else could it be?"

"Pa!" Molly wailed. "It isn't Ezra, is it?" She looked at me, saying, "Ezra isn't deaf! He has a name. And he's not an Indian."

Pa had picked up the paper and was peering at it intently. I couldn't believe I hadn't noticed before that he was having trouble reading. When he had finished, he put his hand on Molly's shoulder and looked at Mr. Beckwith. "What do you know about this?" he asked.

Orrin Beckwith looked flummoxed. "I believe I was given that in western Pennsylvania," he said.

"By who?" I asked.

Orrin Beckwith gave me a wary look, likely because of the anger I could feel creeping into my heart and my voice.

"Who gave it to you?" I insisted.

He shrugged. "I can't say. A man was handing them out. I can't recall what town I was in. I'd forgotten I even had it."

"Where was this show headed to?"

He shrugged again, and looked away from me, to Pa. "What's got you folks so riled?" he asked. When no one answered right off, he said, "Who's this fellow Ezra, anyhow?"

Pa sighed, like the question made him feel sad.

"Not that it's any of my business," Orrin Beckwith added, but it was plain he was curious to know.

Pictures ran through my mind. I saw Ezra leading Molly and me through the forest to his we-gi-wa, a shelter made Shawnee-style with poles and sheets of elm bark, where he was healing Pa's wounds. I saw Ezra teaching me to throw his hunting stick. I saw Ezra cleaning a turkey and making stew and blue biscuits.

I didn't want to tell Orrin Beckwith about Ezra, even if I could have found the words. It seemed to me that Ezra's story belonged to him and to us. Not to Beckwith, someone we'd only just met.

Pa said wearily, "He's our friend. He saved my life when I was caught in a trap. He's not Shawnee, but he took up their ways. Last we knew, he was headed out to the Indian Territory to find his wife's kinfolk."

I was glad Pa didn't say the whole truth, that Ezra's Shawnee wife, Gives-light-as-she-walks, and her unborn baby were killed by a man named Weasel. And that Weasel cut out Ezra's tongue for saying the Shawnees were people just as good as us white folks. I heard the story from Weasel himself, the night he had me hog-tied in his cabin, before I escaped.

Those awful memories never went away, hard as I tried to put them behind me. Pa, Molly, and I didn't speak about Weasel after Ezra left in the spring. Instead, we talked about how Ezra had most likely found his wife's family. We liked to think that the Shawnees welcomed him and took him in. We pictured Ezra happy and peaceful, at last.

But that picture was shattered now. I saw Ezra standing in the bed of a wagon, a sign over his head calling him the White Injun. I imagined people pointing and staring, laughing and poking at him, trying to get him to open his mouth.

"Pa," I said, "I've got to find him."

2

MOLLY STARTED TO CRY then, and Pa's face grew grave. "I understand your feeling, Nathan," he said, "but—"

I interrupted him, something I didn't usually do. "Pa, I want to go."

Pa gave me a tired smile. "I know that. But you're still a boy. And you've already seen more of the hard and ugly side of life than any boy should."

"Pa—"

"Nathan, you heard Mr. Beckwith. He doesn't remember where he was when he learned of the show. It could be anywhere by now."

"I could find it, Pa. I know I could."

Pa sighed. "We don't know that the man in the show *is* Ezra."

I knew in my heart it was Ezra and, looking Pa in the eye, I could tell he knew it, too. I was sure Molly did, also. She raised her tear-streaked face and whispered,

"Ezra helped us, Pa. We *have* to help him. He doesn't have anybody else."

Pa closed his eyes, like he had a pain someplace and was waiting for it to pass. Orrin Beckwith was looking back and forth from one of us to the other, a real interested expression on his face.

"I'd like to help Ezra, too. But just how do you propose I do that?" Pa asked. "Am I going to up and leave the farm with the crop about to come in? Leave you and Molly and the animals? To head off—where?" He spread his hands out to include the whole wide world.

I was trying hard to think of a good answer when Orrin Beckwith spoke up and surprised me. "I might be able to offer a solution to your dilemma," he said.

I looked at him, waiting for him to go on.

"A man can't leave his farm at fall harvesttime, Mr. Fowler. And I'm sure you count on the boy here to help. But if you could spare him for a spell, he could travel with me. I will be passing through the vicinity of western Pennsylvania again, and I've no doubt we could pick up word of this show and where it was headed. It's quite possible he could be back in time to help bring in the crops."

Pa looked startled, then seemed to be thinking it over.

For my part, I had a question. "What do you stand to gain from such an arrangement, Mr. Beckwith?"

Molly gasped at my rudeness. I reckon it was a right bold question, but I had to know. Anyhow, Beckwith didn't appear to be insulted. He was pulling on his chin whiskers and looking squinty-eyed, like he was working something out in his head.

"When I heard you sawing on that fiddle, it got me thinking."

I glanced at Pa, but he didn't seem to notice Beckwith had let slip that I was fiddling instead of working. That, or he didn't mind too much.

"You see," Beckwith went on, "I've discovered I'm not really cut out for this rough traveling. I'd rather do my peddling in bigger towns than the ones you got out here, places where a man can find an inn or a tavern, have a meal, and sleep in a bed. Truth to tell, my plan is to make a stake so I can have my own inn someday."

Here Orrin Beckwith paused and sat himself down. I wondered what his problem had to do with me and my fiddle.

"Now, out here at the edge of civilization, all I have to do is open my pack and folks line up like pigs at the trough, if you'll pardon the expression. But in your larger towns, folks see merchandise like mine all the time. A man needs something to make him stand out in a crowd, make folks want to buy from him and not the other fellow, if you see what I mean."

He was taking a long time getting to it, but I was beginning to see what his point might be. Sure enough, next he said, "If you was to start playing that fiddle when we first pulled into a town, people would gather to listen. That's all I need, is to get 'em close. Once I got 'em in earshot range, I can pull 'em the rest of the way in with my powers of persuasion. I've been told by many a lady that I possess a silver tongue."

Beckwith sat back, looking mighty pleased with himself, at least until he saw Pa's face, and Molly's, and mine, too, I reckon.

"Did I hear right?" I asked. "Did you just call us pigs for wanting to see in your pack?"

Beckwith pushed himself up straight in the chair and mumbled, "No offense meant, you understand. It was merely a manner of speaking."

I almost felt sorry for him then. But I was thinking about his offer. I'd gotten myself to town as often as I could to get fiddle lessons from Eli Tanner. Eli was the best fiddler around, and he won the contest held every year at Whitefield's store. He said I had natural talent and a good ear, and I'd already learned to play a few tunes start to finish. Still, I didn't think I was good enough for what Orrin Beckwith had in mind. I wasn't about to mention it, though.

Pa stood up and said it was time for supper, and that he'd think on it while we ate. We had a somber meal, not like the merry times we used to have with Isaac. I reckon Molly, Pa, and I were all thinking about Ezra and what was going to happen next.

While Molly and I cleaned up, Pa and Orrin Beckwith spoke quietly by the fire. Then Pa sent Molly and me to bed. We could hear Pa and Beckwith talking more as the night grew darker.

My feet itched something awful, and it was peculiar to

think I might be going on a journey, after all. I never thought I'd sleep, what with the itching and the murmur of voices, but I did. I had terrible dreams. In them Ezra was trying to call to me for help.

Next morning, Pa told me it was settled: I was leaving that very day to go with Orrin Beckwith. Beckwith would take me back along his route into Pennsylvania, where he was sure we'd hear news of the traveling show. It all seemed so sudden-like.

The plan, as Pa had just described it, sounded as wiggly as his eyesight. All at once, I had my doubts about it. Pa must have known, because he caught my eye and gave a sideways glance at Molly. Then I knew there was more he wanted to say to me, but not in front of her. I nodded to show I understood.

I looked at Orrin Beckwith, who was settling up with Pa over the cost of Molly's dyes, and felt more than a little uncertain at the prospect of heading off with him. Then I thought of Ezra again, and pushed the uneasiness out of my mind.

Pa caught up with me when I was doing my chores. I'd fed the chickens and Job, our horse, and was milking Golly when Pa came into the barn. I kept my eyes on the stream of milk hitting the pail while he talked.

"Nathan," he said, "I'm of two minds about this thing. I want to help Ezra, but not if it means putting you in danger."

There was silence for a minute, and I looked at Pa. He was rubbing his eyes with the heels of his hands. His shoulders looked droopy. The worry in his mind showed all over his body.

"I can't think what could have happened for Ezra to end up in such a fix," he said.

I had been wondering about the same thing. It bothered me, too. But I'd come up with an explanation in my mind. "Here's how I figure it," I said. "I reckon these show folks tricked him somehow and he couldn't speak up for himself. And since he turned his back on killing and such after he left the army, he wouldn't fight back. That's why he needs help, Pa."

Pa looked thoughtful. "Could be you're right. There's just no telling."

"I expect finding him will be the hardest part," I said, then shrugged. "After that, I'll bring him home with me."

Pa hesitated a minute. "What if he doesn't want to come?"

I looked at him, astonished. "Why wouldn't he want to leave that show? You know how he is about being around people."

"Yes," Pa said gently. "And that includes us, too, Nathan."

"But—"

"Oh, I know Ezra cares for you and Molly and me," Pa went on. "But he's given up on white folks' ways, you know that."

"At least I can get him away from that show, and

then . . ." My voice trailed off. I didn't know what would come next.

Pa shook his head. "Say he *is* with the show against his will. Who's holding him? And what's a boy, even one near grown like yourself, going to do about it?"

I was quiet, thinking. "I reckon I can't know till I get there," I said finally.

Pa looked at me, and in his face I could see how much he wished he could do this instead of me.

"I'm not afraid, Pa," I lied.

"I am," he said, but his voice was so low I wasn't sure I'd heard right.

After a moment he spoke again. "I remember listening to a preacher one time. He said that when a man is faced with a decision, the hard choice is almost always the right one. But I can't figure which is harder, turning my back on Ezra's trouble, or sending you off after him. I keep wondering what your mama would say about all this."

"She'd want me to help Ezra," I said without hesitating a minute. "You know how she was."

"Yes, but she'd rather have died herself than see you come to harm," Pa said.

My eyes blurred with sudden tears, and I tried to blink them away. "Nothing's going to happen to me, Pa." After a moment I added, "Though I wish it was Isaac I was going with, instead of Beckwith."

Pa looked at me curiously. "Beckwith gave me his

word he'll stay with you until you find Ezra. He seems a decent fellow."

I shrugged. I didn't want Pa to change his mind, so I decided not to say any more. But it was like Pa knew how I was feeling.

He sighed and said, "Nathan, there's another reason I'm going to allow you to do this, besides Ezra's needing help."

"What's that?" I asked.

"Ever since that business with Weasel, you've reminded me of a horse I used to have," he said.

"A *horse*?" I repeated. "Which one?"

"I called him Amos," Pa said.

Pa named all his horses out of the Bible, but I didn't recollect one by that name.

"It was before you were born," Pa went on. "I don't know what happened to old Amos before I got him, but whatever it was, it made him skittish. If I raised my hand just to scratch my nose, he'd buck or shy away. Now, you know I'd never strike an animal, but you couldn't have convinced old Amos of that. It didn't matter how kind and gentle I treated him."

Beckwith had as much as called me a pig, and now Pa was saying I reminded him of a horse. I didn't take to being likened to a creature as foolish as the one Pa was describing. I waited to see just what he was getting at.

"I reckon what I'm saying is, I don't want to see that happen to you, son. A man who's suspicious of everybody ends up in a mighty sad and narrow place."

I was struggling to understand. "You said this had something to do with Weasel. Are you saying I'm wrong to be wary of him and his kind?"

"No," Pa said softly. "The trouble comes when you can't see the difference between him and his kind and regular, well-meaning folks."

I waited for him to go on.

"That's why I'm thinking it might do you good to go out in the world a bit. Open your eyes to all the different sorts of people out there."

I stood quiet, trying to let my thoughts settle. Pa was going to let me go after Ezra. That was good, even though I didn't much hold with his reasoning, especially the part about the horse.

Pa reached into his trouser pocket and held something out to me. It was a cloth pouch with a leather drawstring. "Take this," he said. "If you need it, spend it."

I opened the pouch and stared at the five-dollar gold piece. It hardly seemed real. "But, Pa, how—I mean to say, where did it come from?"

"It was your mama's. She was saving it. She always said there'd come a day when we'd have need of it. I reckon she'd want you to have it now."

It made me feel safer, somehow, to have Mama's gift with me, close to my heart. I slipped the pouch over my head and hid it under my shirt so nobody, including Beckwith, would know it was there.

"I hope not to use it," I said. "I'd like for you to get yourself some of those spectacles."

Pa smiled. "Wouldn't that be something?" After a moment he said, "Beckwith's anxious to get on his way, Nathan, so when you're finished here, we'll get you packed up. And then—"

He stopped there. I didn't want to think about saying good-bye till I had to, and I reckon he didn't, either.

"I'll be just a few more minutes," I told him.

When I finished milking Golly, I gave her a pat and let her into the fenced-in pasture. Then I brought Job out to join her. I patted Job's velvety nose and buried my face in his mane for a moment. His warm, familiar smell always comforted me. I murmured in Job's ear something about itchy feet and how I was going on a journey and how I'd see him soon, and he whinnied back, like he got my meaning.

Job was sweet-natured, patient, and hardworking. We were lucky to have him. Weasel had come and stolen him once, along with our mule, Crabapple, and some chickens and piglets. My pet pig, Miz Tizz, had been too big for Weasel to carry off, but that hadn't saved her from his meanness. When I'd found her lifeless body, I'd known right off it was Weasel who'd done it. The memory chilled me even now.

I'd gotten Job back, but we never did see Crabby again. I still missed him and his stubborn ways.

Back at the cabin, Molly took a locket strung on a strip of leather from around her neck and handed it to me. Ezra had made it for her out of bone, with a likeness of her face carved into it.

Then she took a tall black hat from the hook on the wall and placed it on my head. It used to be Ezra's, and I'd told him once how someday I aimed to get me a hat just like it. When he'd gone away in the spring, he'd left Molly the locket with a snip of his hair inside. And he'd left me the hat, along with a message to be happy wearing it.

"Come back soon," Molly said fiercely. "With Ezra." Before I could answer, she turned away and began to wrap some food for me to take on the journey. Her movements were hectic and jerky, and I knew she was trying not to cry.

I fastened the locket around my neck, where it hung along with the pouch that held the gold coin. Having it made me feel even stronger. I *would* return home safe, so Molly'd have her locket back.

I gathered my clothes and considered the matter of how to carry my fiddle so it would be protected. Molly got me a blanket and her worn cradle quilt and we wrapped the fiddle and bow in them, then bundled my clothes around that. We put it all in a basket with shoulder straps and a flap of oiled leather over the top to keep out rain.

And, just like that, it was time to go. Duffy and Winston seemed to sense that something unusual was happening. They stood by, whining, their tails wagging, and I leaned down to scratch their ears while Pa and Beckwith shook hands. When Molly hugged me, she broke down and cried, and I about did, too. Then Pa hugged me hard. We didn't say anything; there was nothing left to say. I pulled Ezra's black hat down low over my eyes.

Duffy and Winston pranced alongside Beckwith and me as we crossed the big pasture. When we reached the edge of the woods, I turned back. Molly and Pa were standing right where we'd left them, and I longed to be standing there, too, waving good-bye to Beckwith. When Duffy and Win left me to race back toward the cabin, I felt near as lonesome as I ever had.

3

I STARTED OUT following Beckwith through the forest, reminding myself to keep a watchful eye for landmarks that would help me find my way when I returned with Ezra. My load was pretty light compared to the huge, oddly shaped pack the peddler had to wrestle with. It slowed him down considerable, as it reached up taller than his head and was forever getting caught on low-hanging branches. Every time it happened, he muttered under his breath—things I reckon Mama would not have wanted me to hear.

I scrambled over a fallen tree and Beckwith tried to follow. He lost his balance and fell backwards. Lying there, waving his arms, he looked as helpless as an overturned beetle.

"Come give a fellow a hand up," he called.

After that he wanted to stop and rest, even though I figured we'd been walking for only a little over an hour. I wasn't halfway tired, but Beckwith took off his pack with a groan and lay down on his back, staring up through the treetops to the clear blue sky. "Someday there will be a road through this godforsaken, infernal wilderness, Nathan," he said. "Peddlers will live a life of ease, traveling by wagon instead of like beasts of burden."

I looked at the dense growth all around us and tried to picture a wagon making its way through. It didn't seem likely. I wondered if Beckwith was a liar, a dreamer, or just plain crazy. Besides, to me the woods weren't godforsaken or infernal, either. They were home.

"I heard of a road that goes across Ohio from western Virginia to Kentucky," I said. "But folks say it's no more than an old Indian trail with some of the trees cut back. Good for travel by foot or on horseback, maybe, but—" I stopped, seeing that Beckwith had something to say on the subject.

"Zane's Trace is what you're talking about," Beckwith said. "Your description's right, but it won't be a mere trail for long. There's wagons on it now, though it's rough going. Folks are going to keep coming this way. Soon there'll be roads, towns, even cities, in this very spot where we're standing."

His words hung for a moment in the still, silent air. Then they were quickly swallowed by the trees and their shadows. The forest was deep and thick and spread on forever. Sitting in the midst of it all, I couldn't see it coming to an end, try as I might.

It was true that we'd got word some new folks were

planning on settling out our way. And every time I went to town, it seemed a new building had sprung up. But, still, I figured the peddler was playing me for a fool.

"You ever been to a big city, Nathan?"

I shook my head.

"Well, you won't see the likes of Philadelphia or Boston on this journey," he went on. "But depending how far you chase after this Ezra fellow, I expect you'll see towns bigger than you can imagine and sights that'll make your hair curl."

He looked like he might start in telling tales to get my hair curling right then and there. Any other time, I might have been curious to hear them, even if they were most likely lies. But I wanted to get moving, toward Ezra.

"How long you reckon before we reach Pennsylvania?" I asked.

"Oh, four or five days' travel, if all goes well. But if there's one thing I've learned about life on the road, it's this: all will *not* go well. It never does."

I hoped he was wrong about that, but what I said was, "Then we best get going."

Beckwith rose with another loud groan and made a big show of settling his pack on his shoulders. Right off, we had to cross a stream, and he cussed considerable about getting his boots wet. I wondered who he complained to before I took up with him. The birds, maybe, or the trees.

We walked for a while without talking, the water squishing in our boots. It felt good on my itchy, swollen feet. I was worried some about what Beckwith would expect of me when we finally reached a town, and after a while I decided to ask. He brightened up as he explained how he figured it would go.

"The first town we come to calls itself Tullyville," he began. "It's near about the same size as the town you're used to, maybe a little bigger. We'll get there tomorrow or the day after. We particularly want the ladies to be out and about, so it's best if we can show up in the middle of the day. Why do we want the ladies around, you might ask?"

I did wonder.

Beckwith gave me a foxy look and said, "Listen sharp, young man, for I'm about to let you in on the tricks of my trade. First of all, you must win over the ladies. Understand that they are out here in the midst of nowhere, cut off from the comforts and trappings of civilization. They hunger for the sight of beauty and color, for the feel of things soft and smooth, for the chance to possess something that will ease the hardship of their lives, or lighten the burden of their labors. A snippet of gay ribbon, a shiny brooch, some flower seeds, a silk shawl—such treasures can help a woman make it through a long, harsh winter."

I could see the truth in what he was saying. I remembered Mama's pleasure in the things she'd been able to buy from Isaac, and Molly's face as she touched and smelled and gazed upon Beckwith's treasures.

"Think of what a cake of sweet-smelling soap means

to a woman making do with the rough stuff she fashions from ashes and lye! Imagine the rewards of a washboard to a woman accustomed to kneeling by a stream to scrub her family's clothes on a rock. To these poor ladies the contents of my pack represent nothing short of hope, Nathan. And hope gives them the courage to go on, to face another year of weevils in the wheat and frightful weather and ailing children and constant weariness."

We were walking up a pretty steady rise, and Beckwith had to stop to catch his breath. He glanced at me, I reckon to see how I was taking his fancy speech. I admit I was impressed by the way the words rolled off his tongue, like maybe he'd said them before just that way.

"Sometimes I carry letters, Nathan, missives from back east, from what used to be home. I watch the women's faces soften when they read those letters, and I know I'm due to make a sale, so grateful are they to get word from their loved ones.

"In the absence of a letter, I try to bring my own happy news, be it jokes or riddles or stories about folks from other places. People love a good story or bit of gossip, Nathan. And—mark this, now—with the women, the judicious use of flattery is a businessman's greatest weapon."

I was trying to work out exactly what he was getting at, but Beckwith winked at me and kept on talking. I got his meaning soon enough.

"It's here that a most delicate balance must be struck. You must speak sincerely enough so that even the drabbest, homeliest, down-on-her-luck creature can believe you mean what you say about the color of her eyes, the fineness of her figure, the skill of her sewing, or the flavor of her cooking. At the same time, you mustn't go so far as to rile the menfolk. There's no point in making a man feel obliged to defend his lady's honor, or any of that nonsense. The object is to make a sale, Nathan, never forget it!"

I didn't say anything, as I was busy pondering the rush of words and trying to decide how I felt about them. It didn't matter if I spoke or not, anyhow. Orrin Beckwith didn't need much encouragement to keep talking.

"Now, the menfolk represent a different challenge, young Nathan, but not so different as you might first suspect. Of course, a man needs tools to use in his work, and to help him protect himself and his family. But it isn't only the fair sex that is prone to vanity, no, sir! You've got to appeal to a fellow's manhood. Then you've got to be alert to any particular need or weakness he's got, so you can offer a remedy. You see what I'm saying here, son?"

The truth was, I did see what he was saying, and I'd concluded I didn't much like it. He had it all worked out how he could skin folks out of their money. He didn't mean to do right by folks, only to make them think he did.

I let my mind go back to the night before, and I could see how Beckwith used every one of his tricks on Molly, and tried 'em on Pa and me, too. It made me feel mad and foolish at the same time. It was good that Molly got dyes to make red and blue for her quilt. But I was glad I hadn't pushed Pa to buy me the Barlow knife.

"A peddler's got to have a keen wit," Beckwith was saying. He gave me another wink and added, "Folks would rather be shaved by a sharp razor than a dull one, Nathan, don't forget it."

I didn't plan on letting anybody shave me one way or another. Maybe Pa wouldn't like to hear me say it, but I didn't trust Beckwith any better now than I had from the first, and I didn't much like him, either. Still, I needed him to get to Ezra.

WE PUSHED ON that afternoon and the next day, with Beckwith doing most of the talking and me trying to keep him moving east as fast as possible. Come dark the second night, the weather turned cold and we sheltered under the boughs of a big spruce tree. I built us a fire, and Beckwith made coffee and heated up beans.

"If we had some ham, we could have ham and eggs, if we had some eggs," he said. Then he peered at me to see how I liked his joke.

I had to smile, in spite of promising myself to stay cautious about the man.

After we ate, Beckwith asked me to play a bit on my fiddle, so I took it out, put some rosin on my bow, and commenced tuning. Eli, my teacher, used to say that fiddlers spent half their time tuning and the other half playing out of tune. I finally got it right, or close enough, anyhow.

I started with a few simple jigs I'd practiced a lot.

Beckwith appeared happy enough with them, even tapping his toe in time to the music. He didn't seem to mind when I began working on some I was only just learning. I did appreciate that. Whenever I practiced at home, Molly made a show of running from the cabin with her hands over her ears. Pa said she was just teasing, but I wasn't altogether sure.

I reckon between the fiddle music and the crackling of the piney wood I'd gathered for the fire, we were making a fair racket. So when a man's voice came from the inky shadows outside the firelight, I pretty near jumped out of my britches.

"Well, well," the voice said. "I knew you'd turn up sooner or later. Bad luck always does."

I was on my feet quicker than a scalded cat. But Orrin Beckwith just leaned forward, stirred the fire with a stick, and said calmly, "You're the one turned up. I figure that makes *you* the bad luck."

The man who had spoken stepped out of the darkness and into the ring of light from our fire. He wore no hat, and his white hair stood out kind of wild. I had the thought that his head looked like a dandylion flower that's gone to seed.

"You've got an answer for everything, haven't you, peddler? Well, answer me this: how come I was sicker'n two pukin' dogs after taking that medicine you sold me?"

Beckwith shrugged and said, "Reckon you'd have been a lot sicker without it. Might even be dead." Then he dumped his coffee, wiped the cup on his trousers, poured a fresh cup, and held it out to the dandylion feller. "If you don't come in by the fire, old man, you'll be sick again. And this time you won't have anybody to blame but your own fool self."

The man came closer, set his pack down, and took the cup from Beckwith. After a long slurp, he made a face and said, "If this is coffee, I'll have tea. If this is tea, then I'll have the coffee."

"Call it whatever you like," Beckwith answered. "It's all there is."

I'd been standing still as a stone, watching and listening real close, sure there was going to be trouble.

"Who's this young fellow?" the man asked Beckwith. "And why is he glaring at me like he figures I just finished up murdering ten people with my bare hands?"

"He's kinda nervy," Beckwith said matter-of-factly. "He'll settle down soon enough, once he sees you're too wore out to swat a fly."

I sat then, though I reckon I was scowling at the both of them for talking about me like I wasn't right there.

Beckwith went on, "I'm willing to overlook you coming here and accusing me wrongful if you got something to contribute to our little gathering. A smoke of tobacco, perhaps? Or"—he sounded hopeful—"some whiskey?"

The man shook his head, mournful-like. "Whiskey would indeed be a comfort on a night such as this. But it appears I'll have to make do with your company instead. Yours and the fiddler boy's, that is."

He sat and looked across the fire at me. "Got a name, fiddler boy?"

I couldn't see any good reason not to answer, so I said, "Nathan Fowler, sir."

The man nodded. "Joseph R. Honeywell, artist, portrait painter, and silhouette cutter. Have you any money, Nathan Fowler?" It was his turn to look hopeful.

"No." I didn't see any reason to tell him, or Beckwith, either, about Mama's gold coin. Then I repeated it louder. "No."

"You sure 'bout that?" Honeywell asked.

I nodded.

" 'Cause if you've got some money, I can make a likeness of you so real it'll convince your own mother she bore twins."

Orrin Beckwith let out a guffaw at that. "Don't believe a word this scoundrel says, Nathan," he cautioned. "And when he leaves, as I sincerely hope he will, check your pockets and count your fingers and toes to make sure they're all present and accounted for."

Honeywell pretended to be affronted. "I don't have to sit here and have my honesty questioned," he said.

"That's right," Beckwith agreed. "You don't. And if you want to see how much we'll miss you when you go, stick your finger in the creek over there, pull it out, and look at the hole."

I'd never heard grown men carry on so, trading insults back and forth. I was trying to remember all they said, so I could tell Molly and Pa about it.

Honeywell turned to me and said, "You there, grinning like a roast possum, how'd you come to take up with a ne'er-do-well like Orrin Beckwith?"

Quick as I could, I explained about playing my fiddle so as to draw a crowd for Beckwith, and about Ezra and the traveling show I was in search of. "Have you seen or heard tell of such a show, Mr. Honeywell?"

Honeywell put his hands behind his head, stretched out his legs, and looked toward the sky. "My boy, in my travels I've seen exhibitions and performances of every sort and description. I've seen a creature called an Al-Bi-No, who had the palest skin you ever saw, and pure white hair, and pink eyes. I've seen Siamese twins, which is two whole people growed together as one. Here, look, I made a sketch of them so's I'd never forget the sight."

Honeywell reached for his pack. There was a wooden stand tied to the outside, which I figured might be where he placed a painting while he worked on it. Inside were a quiver of brushes of all sizes, and rolled-up canvases. He unrolled one and held it up. It took me a while to make sense of what I was looking at, which was two men hitched together somehow so they had two heads but shared a body. It made my stomach feel a little funny, but I couldn't stop looking at it.

"Did you make that up or see it for real?" I asked.

"Oh, it was real as real can be," Honeywell answered. "I've also seen an orang-u-tang, a mummy, a mermaid, a midget, a giant, a dwarf, and a lady with chin whiskers down to her waist. I've seen a man with no arms who played the fiddle better than you and shot arrows with his toes. I've seen pigeons, horses, dogs, and bears trained to sing and dance and count to ten. I've seen a two-headed calf, a five-legged pig, an Arabian camel, an African zebra, and a laughing hyena. Once I paid good money to a gypsy fortune-teller who looked at the flat of my hand and said I would die young but rich. Ha!"

He took another sip of coffee, spit into the fire, then added, "I did see a man in a show who was deef and dumb. Folks wrote down questions on a slate and he answered 'em in sign language like an Injun. I don't suppose that's who you're looking for?"

Feeling dazed, I shook my head. Could Honeywell be telling the truth? Had he really seen such things? The idea made my head swim. It sounded like there were all sorts of traveling shows, not just one, as I'd imagined. That made finding Ezra seem a lot harder.

And even though it shamed me, I was curious to see some of the things Honeywell had spoken of.

Right about then, I began to feel plain wore out from the travelin' and from all the talk I'd heard that day, first from Beckwith and then from Honeywell. I reckoned talking was about all they ever did.

I wrapped my fiddle in my pack, spread out my blanket, set Ezra's hat down alongside it, and said good night. Beckwith and Honeywell blathered for a right long time after that, I reckon. I heard part of a story about a catfish that walked on dry land and one about a man who came back to life when his coffin fell off a wagon and busted open.

It was no wonder I had some peculiar dreams. In one, that dead man from the wagon came right into our camp, sat down, and played my fiddle. In another, a trained bear talked in sign language and tried to put his paws around my neck for a dance.

When I woke in the morning, Beckwith was already talking. Or maybe he'd never stopped. He had fixed more coffee and beans, and he and Honeywell jawed about where they were headed next. Beckwith allowed as how we were going east, and suggested that Honeywell point himself to the west, north, or south. "No sense in folks having to choose between spending their money on my goods or yours," he said with a shrug.

Honeywell appeared to agree. He shouldered his own pack and looked at me. "I hope you find the gentleman you're looking for," he said. "In the meantime, if you get tired of listening to this rascal's lies, look me up. I'm a better cook, when I've got the fixin's, and I could stand the company."

I was surprised by the offer, and even a little bit tempted. Honeywell came off a decent feller. But I needed to stick with Beckwith, who was headed east, toward Ezra. Beckwith was a scoundrel, but I'd be all right as long as I kept that in mind.

"Thank you, sir," I told Honeywell. "I hope you find lots of folks who want their likeness made."

He nodded. To Beckwith, he said, "How far's the next town west?"

"It seems farther than it is," Beckwith said with a grin, "but once you get there, you'll find it ain't."

Honeywell scowled. "Thank you kindly for that useful information. When I get there, reckon I'll sell tickets to your funeral and make me a bundle."

Beckwith laughed and wished Honeywell luck, and then we went our separate ways. It wasn't till the sun was getting high overhead that I reached up to touch the pouch around my neck—and discovered that it was gone.

I CRIED OUT in dismay, and Beckwith turned around to see what was wrong.

"My money!" I said. Too late, I remembered I didn't want to tell Beckwith I had money, but it didn't matter anymore. "My pa gave me a five-dollar coin, and it's gone!"

Beckwith looked at me and shook his head sadly. "I tried to warn you about Honeywell. Didn't I tell you to keep a sharp eye on your fingers and toes and whatever else you got?"

"You mean to say he took my money?" I asked. Then, before Beckwith could answer, I said, "No. He couldn't have. He didn't know I had it. The only one who knew was me."

"Not true, Nathan," Beckwith said solemnly. "*I* knew."

I was almost too astonished to speak. "You did?" I shook my head in bewilderment. "But how?"

Beckwith gave a little smile. "I suspected it from the

first, the way you were always foolin' with something hanging around your neck. I saw your sister give you that locket, but there was something else, too. Then last night around the fire I knew for sure. You practically came right out and made a pronouncement."

"I didn't say any such thing!" I cried.

"You didn't have to," Beckwith replied. "Honeywell asked if you had money and you said no. You're not a practiced liar, Nathan. Your face was enough to give you away to anybody who was paying attention. But your hand went to that string around your neck, and right then I knew not only that you had money but also exactly where you were keeping it. I've no doubt Honeywell saw the same thing."

And I'd thought Honeywell was a decent feller. I was too disgusted with myself to speak.

Beckwith went on. "People tell things about themselves without meaning to, Nathan. When you're living by your wits, you learn to read people just like you read a book. You hear the things people don't know they're saying."

To heck with reading people like a book, I thought. You could pretty much count on them being low-down and shifty.

Beckwith gave a little shrug. "Honeywell's no different from most men. He saw an opportunity and took it."

In my mind, I was remembering my dream. Someone *had* been reaching around my neck. It wasn't any trained bear, though, but Honeywell. Now, because of my stupidity, Mama's gold piece was gone. Pa could have used it to buy himself some spectacles, but he'd given it to me and told me to use it wisely. My belly ached.

Beckwith had resumed walking. He called back loudly, "Come along, Nathan, time's a-wasting. Look at it this way: you learned a valuable lesson today, one you're not likely to forget."

I forced my feet to follow along behind him, although my mind was filled with fury at Honeywell, and at myself, and at Beckwith, too, for his cheery advice about learning lessons.

We kept on, heading pretty near due east. I reckon I wasn't very good company. The knowledge of Honeywell's trickery gnawed at me. I wanted to go after him, grab him by *his* neck, and get back my money.

Then I'd think of Ezra, and make myself keep going. But something had changed. Having Mama's gift next to my heart had made me feel strong and confident, and without it I felt shaky and unsure. I touched Molly's locket, and thought longingly of her and Pa and home.

✽

As we worked our way east, we began to travel through more settled areas. Where Pa and Molly and I might go weeks without seeing another soul, Beckwith and I began to meet up with folks quite regular. Beckwith tried to make a sale to everyone we saw, and almost always made one. Every farm we stopped at made me more homesick, and I wondered how Pa was making out without me.

I looked hard at every tall, dark-haired man to see if he might be Ezra, but he never was. I asked everyone we met if they'd come across a traveling show of monstrosities, curiosities, and whatnot, but no one had. Then, on the fourth day, as we reached the outskirts of Tullyville, we came to a handbill tacked onto a tree. It wasn't the same one Beckwith had brought to our cabin, but it had the same flavor about it. It read:

BRAVE LADIES AND GENTLEMEN
COME IF YOU DARE!

SEE THE SAVAGE DEVIL-BEAST OF BORNEO
BIGGER THAN A GRIZZLY,
**MEANER THAN A NEST OF RATTLERS,
WILDER THAN A PACK OF WOLVES!
THE MOST TERRIFYING CREATURE
EVER TO WALK THE EARTH!!**
THE DEVIL-BEAST OF BORNEO WILL MAKE

ONE APPEARANCE
and ONE appearance only
8 P.M. TONIGHT
☞ TOWN HALL ☜
PRICE OF ADMISSION 10 CENTS!!
DO NOT MISS THIS ONCE-IN-A-LIFETIME OPPORTUNITY!!

Then, in real small print, it said:

❀ ATTEND AT YOUR OWN RISK. ❀
ALL PRECAUTIONS WILL BE TAKEN TO PROTECT THE AUDIENCE.

Funny, but it was that last part written small that tickled my imagination the most. For the first time since it happened, I quit brooding about the loss of my money. Feeling curious, I asked Beckwith, "What kind of critter you reckon it is?"

He chuckled and said, "Likely a bear or a wildcat they got tricked out to scare folks. Could be they added horns or feathers or whatnot. Could even be a person wearing a fur skin, I suppose, if they got clever enough."

"You mean to say it ain't for real?" I asked.

"I'll sprout wings and fly to France if it is," Beckwith answered.

He spoke so sure of himself, it was downright annoying at times. I thought it likely there could be a beast he hadn't heard of. "You ever been to this Borneo place?" I asked him.

"No," Beckwith answered. "But I don't need to see a rat to smell one."

Well, maybe so. But, still . . . The truth was, the idea of that Devil-Beast had got me wound-up.

"Nevertheless," he went on, "it's bound to be an entertaining spectacle. And that, Nathan, is bad luck for us."

"How so?"

"People love a spectacle. They're sure to be handing

over money to see this beast tonight. What we've got to do is see how many of their dimes we can get to first."

I couldn't help thinking about the Devil-Beast of Borneo as Beckwith and I walked the rest of the way into town and up the dusty main street. The handbills about it were posted on every storefront and hitching post. People gathered around to read them, pointing and speculating. It seemed every snatch of conversation I overheard was about the upcoming show. Everybody appeared to be as excited as I was. None of them talked about it being a trick, so what made Beckwith so almighty sure of himself?

We walked down the main street until we came to a tavern called the Spotted Hog. Here Beckwith took off his pack and said, "Start playing, Nathan. Something lively. And loud."

This was the first town we'd come to. It was the moment I'd been secretly dreading. I'd never played in front of folks before, only just Molly, Pa, Eli Tanner, and Beckwith. I'd heard good fiddlers and knew I wasn't one of them yet. There was so much feeling in Eli's music that it made folks weep. So far I had to work hard just to get the notes right. Eli said the feeling would come later. I hoped so. At the moment, I was more than half afraid people would laugh or even jeer.

After I tuned and rosined, I began to play, though my hands were shaking some. Beckwith did a little jig to catch folks' attention, and to my surprise people began to drift our way. Soon there was a fair-sized crowd gathered around, mostly ladies and children. Beckwith gave me a sign to stop, and he started talking. Just as he had with Molly, he opened by asking a riddle.

"I have a question for the smartest youngster in the crowd," he called out.

Three young boys and one girl all stepped up. The girl hollered, "That's me!"

"If three crows are sitting on a fence and you shoot one and kill it, how many are left?"

"Two!" shouted the children.

"Not at all!" cried Beckwith. "For the other two would fly away!"

Laughter and groans came from the crowd, and Beckwith tried a couple of the same riddles he'd used with me and Molly. It made me feel a little better that nobody else figured out the one about the cow turning grass to milk and butter, either.

Then he asked, "What has four legs up and four legs down, is soft in the middle and hard all around?"

The little girl who had spoken up before shrieked and said, "The Devil-Beast of Borneo!"

Everyone had a good laugh about that, and then a boy about my same age called out, "I know that one. The answer's a bed!"

Beckwith tipped his hat to the boy and told him how smart he was, and soon proceeded to say the boy would need a good shaving razor before too long. Beckwith said he just might have such a thing in his pack.

I stood by and watched him work his tricks on the crowd. He showed the young children little carved wooden animals and tops. He held up hair ribbons and combs and shawls and soaps to the ladies and allowed them to look and touch and smell. When men came from the tavern to see what was going on, out came tools and elixirs and Barlow knives and more.

I saw the longing in their faces, the wanting in their outstretched hands, and watched as Beckwith made one sale after another. Some folks stood back, their arms crossed over their chests, which I was beginning to see meant they were holding back, trying not to be charmed by Beckwith's "silver tongue." A few folks murmured about saving their money for the show that evening, but even so it seemed to me we were doing a pretty good business.

When the crowd had gone, Beckwith counted up his money. He'd taken in a hodgepodge of dimes, half dimes, cents, half cents, shillings, ninepence, coppers, and Spanish reales, which made figuring difficult, leastways for me. But Beckwith claimed we'd made well over three dollars.

A woman waited there with us till we put our packs back together. She fancied a set of tin cups, and had offered us corn bread, a piece of ham, and a dozen eggs in trade. She'd told us we could sleep in the barn, too, long as we didn't mind the rooster crowing early in the morning.

We followed her home, made the trade, and settled our belongings in the hayloft. Then I made a small fire outside.

While the ham and eggs were cooking, Beckwith rubbed his chin whiskers contentedly. "All in all, that was a much more profitable afternoon than I'd anticipated, Nathan. Your fiddling drew us a fine crowd. I think I can spare two thin dimes, and I'm curious to see the tomfoolery myself. How 'bout you and I take in the show tonight?"

I had tried to tell myself I didn't much care, but now that it looked like we were going, I could admit it: I wanted to see that show awful bad.

Why should I believe Beckwith against a whole town full of people? I wished I could tell Molly and Pa I was going to see the savage Devil-Beast of Borneo with my very own eyes!

6

IT WAS GETTING ON dark when Beckwith and I headed to the show. Everybody in town seemed to be in the street, talking excitedly and going in the same direction. The crowd included men, women, children, even babies and old folks hobbling along on canes and crutches.

A long line had formed at the entryway to the town hall. A big, red-faced man was keeping folks in place. "No need to push and shove, ladies and gentlemen," he called out. "There's room for all, and I assure you, the Devil-Beast won't make its appearance until everyone is seated."

A skinny man with dark, greasy hair poking out from under his felt hat was taking money. Some people, who I expect were lacking dimes, brought food or other items to trade. I didn't see the skinny man turn anybody away.

Beckwith and I were getting close to the entrance when suddenly a wild and terrible roar came from inside.

It sounded like no animal I'd ever heard, not wolf or coyote or wildcat, either. A shiver shot right through me and down my back. People screamed, and some children began to cry.

The big, red-faced man shouted, "Remain calm, ladies and gentlemen. Do not panic! You are perfectly safe. The Devil-Beast is restrained by the strongest chains and bars known to man. Escape is impossible. Keep moving now, so the show can begin."

The crowd was making its own roar, and it was growing louder and more high-pitched. I glanced at Beckwith, who was grinning from ear to ear and appeared to be enjoying himself immensely. I checked the expressions on the faces of the other men. Their eyes looked feverish with excitement and fear. Some of them fingered pistols they carried on their hips.

Beckwith winked when he gave the skinny man two dimes, and we went inside. I was relieved to see that all the front seats were already taken. A few lanterns hanging from the roof beams cast a dim light. The front of the room was closed off by a curtain, so folks in the audience couldn't see what was behind it.

Beckwith motioned for me to join him in a row about halfway back. He was looking all around the room, smiling widely at anybody who looked back. I couldn't tear my eyes from that curtain hanging in the front, couldn't stop thinking about what was behind it. Once, when the crowd noise sank low for a minute, I was sure I heard the rattle of chains.

It was pitch black out by the time everybody got in and settled on a seat, and it wasn't much lighter inside. I looked toward the back of the hall and saw the skinny man close the door. I reckoned the show was about to begin, and I felt my heart start thumping.

The red-faced man stepped from behind the curtain wearing a black hat, a bright, stripy tie, and a gentleman's jacket. The crowd hushed all at once. In the sudden quiet, I could almost hear their eager breath and their hearts beating along with mine. Put together, we were like one great hungry beast waiting to be fed.

"Ladies and gentlemen," the man began, "thank you for your patience. I promise you it will be well rewarded. At great peril to life and limb, we have brought to you from darkest, far-off Borneo the most astounding—"

At that moment we heard a loud clanking of chains and a screeching sound like metal ripping. Then there came a crash, another horrible roar, and the sounds of a fearsome scuffle behind the curtain, followed by a scream that made my blood run cold. The red-faced man stopped his speech and froze solid as an icicle, his eyes bugging wide with fear.

A gasp arose from the audience. The curtain was ripped aside and the skinny man appeared. His hair was wild and rumpled, his clothing torn and covered in blood. It was a terrible sight. "Run for your lives!" he shouted. "The Devil-Beast has escaped!"

I never in my life saw such an uproar as followed. Everybody was shrieking and hollering and bawling at once. Folks ran for the door, pushing and shoving, leaping over seats and each other, nearly stepping on a few poor unfortunates who had fallen or been knocked down in the rush.

I was too scared to move right at first. When I finally gathered my wits and looked for Beckwith, I was astonished to see him standing beside me, laughing so hard, tears were spilling down his face. I wondered if I might have struck up company with a madman.

"Come on!" I urged him. "We got to run for our lives!"

He just bent over and laughed harder. I didn't intend for us to be the ones eaten or torn apart by the Devil-Beast. I grabbed Beckwith's arms and pretty near dragged him out of the hall and onto the street.

People were racing off in all directions, and their screams still filled the air. I looked every which way for the Devil-Beast, but it was nowhere in sight. There wasn't any sign of the red-faced man, or the skinny one, either. I pulled Beckwith along behind me. I was headed toward the barn, which was the only place I knew to go.

I figured to get us where it was safe. Later I'd sort out what in tarnation had got into Beckwith. That was my thinking, anyway.

Suddenly a man in front of us stopped and looked around. Then he bellowed in outrage, "Wait just a minute here. There ain't no savage Devil-Beast, escaped or not. We've been hoaxed! Where's those fellers took our money?"

Some of the others quit their running, too, and began talking. Then one of them looked our way. "You there," he said, pointing to Beckwith. "What's so blamed funny?"

Another man said, "Maybe he's in on this here little trick."

Then more voices joined in and became a chorus. "These two showed up in town just today, same as those other two."

"Likely they're all in it together!"

"Reckon they've got explaining to do."

Then the whole bunch of them came after us.

7

QUICKER'N IT TAKES to tell about it, we were sur-
rounded by a mob of angry-looking townsfolk. Some of
the men had their hands on their pistols, I noticed. I felt
little bumps rise up on my arms. People said that meant a
goose just walked over where your grave is going to be
someday, but I knew better. It meant I was scared. Till
right that minute, I didn't know that you can taste fear,
sharp and bitter on your tongue.

"Let's search 'em, see if they got our money," a man
close to us cried.

"Yeah, search 'em!" others agreed.

I looked at Beckwith. He wasn't laughing anymore,
but he didn't look near as scared as I felt. "Gentlemen,
please," he said, "if you'll allow me to explain, I assure
you—"

But a man with a tangled black and gray beard wasn't
having any of it. He busted in, saying, "Enough with the

fancy talk, mister. We'll do the assurin' around here from now on."

Two other men drew their pistols and pointed them, one at me and one at Beckwith. It wasn't the first time I'd had a gun trained on me; Weasel had done the same with a rifle the night he captured me. But I don't reckon it's a feeling you ever quite get used to. I put my hands in the air before anybody even said to do it, and stood still as a rabbit that's seen the shadow of a hawk passing overhead.

"You," the man who was covering Beckwith said, "hands up, like the boy's."

From the corner of my eye I could see Beckwith give a little shrug, then obey the command.

"Let's see what they got on 'em," the bearded man said. He stepped closer to Beckwith and nodded to a littler man with bushy red hair who was standing near me. "You search the boy, Frank," he said.

"There's no need for that," Beckwith said. "We'll turn our pockets out for you, and you'll find no treasure trove of dimes, I assure—" He gasped and doubled over in pain as the bearded man kicked him in the leg.

"What did I say about assurin'?" the bearded man asked.

Without moving my head, I glanced over and saw a little flicker of satisfaction cross his face. It wasn't new to me that some folks found pleasure in causing pain to another human being, though I didn't think I'd ever understand it. I didn't have time to ponder it right then, though. I was too busy trying to look harmless and follow orders. I wanted to get myself and Beckwith out of the mess we were in and out of Tullyville altogether as soon as possible. I didn't favor the idea of being searched at gunpoint by a stranger, but I wasn't going to argue about it, either.

First the red-haired man reached out and took my hat, the one Ezra had given me, and after looking inside threw it down in the dirt of the road. I bit my lip, hard, and kept quiet. Then the man started at my neck, searching for what I might have hidden under my clothes. Right off he felt the bone locket Ezra had made with the likeness of Molly's face. He yanked it hard enough that the leather string broke. He examined it, scowled, and threw it to the ground beside the hat.

I was plenty mad about that, but I didn't let my anger make me stupid. I kept my wits about me, as Pa had taught me to do. I stood cold and still while the man patted me all over my chest, my arms, and my legs. He felt in my pockets and made me untie my boots and take them off.

When he'd finished, his voice was harsh with disappointment as he announced to the others, "He ain't got nothin' but the clothes on his back."

The bearded man was still working on Beckwith. He found the leather purse where Beckwith had put the money we'd made that afternoon. He dumped it into his hand and peered at it. There were lots of coins there, but not near as many as the little man with greasy hair had taken in at the show. The bearded man seemed angry as he motioned to Beckwith to take off his boots.

Beckwith bent down, untied the laces, and pulled off one boot, then the other. He turned each one upside down and shook it to show there was nothing inside. Then he stood in the street in his stocking feet, his none-too-clean big toe poking out the end of his right sock. His expression said, plain as if he spoke out loud, *I told you so.*

But the bearded man wasn't giving up. "Take off the socks, too," he said.

Beckwith's little smile wavered for a moment. He pulled his mouth back into a grin and said, "My socks? Surely you don't believe there could be a passel of dimes hidden in these wretched garments?"

The bearded man moved his foot as if he meant to give Beckwith another kick to the shins, and I felt myself wince. I wanted to tell him to take off the socks so's they'd be satisfied and leave us alone.

Slowly Beckwith reached down and pulled off his right sock, the one that needed darning, and handed it to the bearded man. It appeared fairly stiff with sweat and grime, and the man made a face when he touched it, then dropped it to the ground. A month of Sundays seemed to pass before Beckwith got the other sock off and handed it over. This one hung heavier from his hand, and when the bearded man took it, a smile spread across his face.

"Well, now, what have we here?" he asked. His voice

was full of pretend surprise. In one hand he held the sock up for the crowd to see. Then he made a big ceremony out of emptying it into the palm of his other hand.

Out came a pouch made of homespun cloth, tied with a leather drawstring. The bearded man made another big show of opening the pouch to see what was in it. But I didn't have to look. I knew it was my pouch with my mama's five-dollar gold piece inside.

8

MY EARS FILLED with a loud roaring. I was about knocked off my feet by the fury I felt at Beckwith's treachery. I couldn't believe I'd taken his word that Honeywell was the culprit. I should have known better. So much strong feeling brought me close to crying, and I tried to get ahold of myself.

"You see?" Beckwith said, speaking to the crowd. "No ill-gotten gains. Just the hard-earned savings of a poor peddler, my protection against a rainy day or a stretch of bad luck."

I about choked at that, but the crowd grew quiet. Then somebody shouted, "If he's a peddler, where's his pack? Could be the money's there."

The others grew restless again until Beckwith spoke up. "My pack is in the barn of one of your kind neighbors. You're welcome to go search it. But surely you can see there has been no time for me to go there to hide your money. I'm sorry, folks. You *have* been hornswoggled, but not by us. The boy and I were victims, too. Those two scoundrels who perpetrated the hoax are no doubt on their way to a safe haven they established well ahead of time, and we are left to contemplate our own foolishness."

This little speech by Beckwith brought grumbles from the crowd, but at least they appeared convinced that Beckwith and I weren't the ones who'd swindled them. The bearded man thrust the leather purse and the cloth pouch into Beckwith's hand. Then he tried to rouse the group to chase after the two showmen, but it seemed most of the anger had given way to embarrassment and chagrin. It looked to me like they just wanted to go home and forget the whole thing. I watched them drift off until it was only Beckwith and me standing in the street.

I made my eyes burn into him until he looked my way. To my astonishment, he *smiled* at me. Then he shrugged and held out the pouch. "It was too easy to pass up, son. No harm done, you agree?"

My voice was cold as I said, "I'm no son to you, so don't call me that. You're nothing like my pa. You're nothing but a low-down crook."

Beckwith sighed deeply. "Nathan, Nathan. Don't get yourself in a lather over this."

I could scarcely believe he was talking like *I* was the one acting unreasonable.

"Why, we're lucky to be alive. It was only due to my quick thinking and fast talking that we *are* alive."

I let out a bitter laugh. "I reckon I'm supposed to forget about you stealing my money and thank you for saving my life, when it was mostly your fool snickering that put us in hot water in the first place?"

There was a moment of silence. Beckwith, seeing that his smiles and shrugs weren't working on me, dropped the wheedling tone. His voice grew impatient. "Nathan, you're not a child; you said as much yourself. In this life, a man has to get what he can, however he can. You can be a lamb or you can be a wolf. Eat or get eaten. Take or get taken.

"If you're as smart as I think you might be, you've learned something tonight. If not"—he shrugged again—"well, like I always say, the wolves never have to look far for an easy meal."

He picked up his socks and boots and walked off barefoot in the direction of the barn. I stood there for a while, feeling rooted as a willow tree on a riverbank. Finally I leaned down and picked up my hat, brushed it off, and put it back on my head. I was glad to see that Molly's locket was still in one piece after the rough treatment it had gotten. I retied the leather string around my neck, then pulled on my boots and followed Beckwith.

I didn't plan on keeping up company with him. The way I figured it, not only didn't I like him, I didn't need him. I had my gold piece back. I'd be able to move faster without him slowing me down. We'd already made it to western Pennsylvania. I could go around asking about the traveling show myself.

But my pack was in the barn alongside his, and I

wasn't about to leave my fiddle for him to sell or give to some other boy to play for the crowds. Besides, there was a good bit of food left back at the barn. I aimed to get me a proper night's sleep and fill up my belly in the morning before parting company with the peddler. A wolf wouldn't pass up the chance for an easy meal, and I didn't aim to be a sheep any longer.

As I walked, I tried to puzzle out everything that had happened. I'd wanted to believe in the Devil-Beast of Borneo, and hadn't wanted to believe Beckwith when he said it would be nothing but a trick. I'd believed Beckwith when he told me Honeywell was a thief, but it turned out Beckwith was a thief and a liar both.

I couldn't seem to get my feet under me when it came to people. Beckwith claimed to read folks like a book, but whenever I tried it, the words got wiggly and I read 'em all wrong.

Pa had sent me out to open my eyes to the whole wide world, and I reckon I had. Far as I could tell, it was full of scoundrels, cheats, and liars.

9

WHEN I GOT BACK to the barn, Beckwith was wrapping himself in his blanket and settling down for the night. I said to him, "I don't believe I'll be traveling with you anymore, Mr. Beckwith. But before we part company, I'd like to buy one of those Barlow knives you got. I'll pay with my gold coin and you can give me back the difference."

Beckwith nodded and said, "I'll sell you the Barlow, but I've got to keep my small coins for making change."

I shook my head and laughed at the gall of the man. "You don't reckon I'm going to give you my whole five dollars for a knife, do you?"

He looked offended and answered, "Of course not." He spoke as if he'd never think of cheating a body.

"Simply cut off part of your precious coin equal to the value of the knife," he said.

I'd heard of people doing what he was talking about. Gold was gold; it didn't matter if it was all in one piece or not. But somehow I didn't like the idea of cutting into Mama's coin. I'd wanted to return it whole to Pa. Still, if I was to be out on my own, I'd need the knife. I'd need it to fashion tools, to make snares to capture food, and to cut branches for firewood and roasting spits.

And, after what had happened with the townsfolk that night, I realized how suddenly a person can find himself neck-deep in trouble. I'd need a weapon to protect myself.

"How do you go about making a cut like that?" I asked.

"You figure it the best you can," Beckwith said. "I've got the tools for it. You can do it yourself, so's you'll be satisfied I'm not cheating you."

Then he yawned and said, "I reckon it can wait till morning, though." He gave me his foxy grin and added, "Unless you're figuring on cutting my throat during the night . . ." He let out a guffaw at that, and I could hear the insult in it, like he knew I'd never do it. He rolled over with another loud yawn and closed his eyes.

He had me pegged for a sheep, but right then I thought I could have wrung his scrawny neck with my bare hands. Instead, I spread out my blanket as far away from him as I could get, slipped the pouch holding Mama's coin into my boot, and lay down on the straw.

Sleep was slow in coming. It didn't matter how many times I told myself I was better off on my own, I was worried about setting out alone. Maybe a thief and a cheat didn't make the best company, but Beckwith *was* company, and the world seemed a large and lonely place to me.

When morning came at last, I made sure to get a bellyful of breakfast. Then Beckwith and I settled down to the matter of the knife. I said I wanted the biggest one he had and he took it from his pack, saying it would cost me an even dollar. He claimed he was giving me a bargain, making the price a nice round number so as to make it easier for me to figure where to cut.

I was about to try and cut into Mama's beautiful, shiny coin with my knife when Beckwith stopped me. "You'll lose gold to shavings that way. Use these."

He handed me a small hammer and a chisel. I positioned the chisel carefully and hit it with the hammer, taking off what I figured to be a fifth of the coin. Beckwith watched me as I worked, talking the whole while.

"That coin's known as a half eagle. It's soft and easy to cut, bein' gold. Some coins are a lot harder."

I hated to ruin the pretty pictures it had on it. Beckwith's share was part of a lady's head on one side, and on the other, part of an eagle's wing. When I handed it to him, he pocketed it without making any comment.

Then he reached into his pack, took out a sheath, and gave it to me. "It won't be any good to you wrapped up in your pack," he said gruffly. "You got to have it where it's handy."

Then he gave me a couple of eggs he'd boiled up hard

that morning. The man was full of surprises. Just when I had him figured for a purebred louse, he had to go and do something nice. It was exasperating, in a way.

"Thanks," I said grudgingly. I cut a piece off the rope tying my pack together, put it through the loop in the sheath, and hung it from my waist. I liked the way it felt. "I reckon I'll be going now," I said.

"Safe travels, Nathan. I hope you find your friend and meet with no further mishaps."

"Safe travels to you, too," I mumbled. I was feeling confused by his kindness, and I had to remind myself of his lying and thieving ways.

The sun was just coming up in the east and I headed toward it. I walked steady, telling myself how good it was to be traveling without Beckwith slowing me down. I came to a little town that wasn't much more than a general store and a livery stable, and asked around. But no one there had heard of any such show as I described.

I made camp that night by a stream, built myself a fire, and cooked a little ham. It was awful quiet without Beckwith's eternal talk. I was thinking how nice it would be if Duffy and Winston were there, curled up beside me. People were altogether too shifty and unpredictable, whereas a dog was straightforward in its dealings. You could count on a dog.

I was just warming up to this line of thinking when I heard the snap of a twig. I jumped up and reached for my knife, and there stood Beckwith with his foxy grin spread wide across his face. "You'll find it ain't easy to get shed of somebody when you're both traveling by foot and going in the same general direction," he observed.

"I reckon not," I said, returning my knife to its sheath. "I heard tell bad luck has a way of showing up. And here you are."

His grin grew bigger, and I smiled back in spite of myself. "Come on and set," I said. "Here I was, wishing for four-legged company, and, sure enough, up walks a skunk."

I was pretty proud of that comment. Beckwith laughed and put down his pack with his usual groaning and carrying-on.

So the peddler and I fell in together again, though I was warier of him than before. We stopped at a few farms along the way to do some peddling, and on the third day we came to a small village. After I'd fiddled and drawn a crowd, I stood back and watched Beckwith work. I had to admire his talent.

Once Beckwith had made his sales, I took out the handbill featuring the show Ezra was part of. "Anybody heard tell of such a thing?" I asked.

It turned out the show had come through town just two days before and folks were still full of talk about it. Never in all their born days, as they told it, had they seen such peculiar sights.

"It was enough to give a body nightmares," one lady said with a shudder.

My heart began to pound against my rib bones. "Did they still have a man who—who didn't speak?" I asked.

"One they called a"—I stopped, hating to say the words—"a White Injun?"

"You mean the savage without a tongue?" a man said. "He's part of it. He's downright creepy, he is."

"He ain't human," another man put in.

"Same for all of 'em," said someone else. "Sent straight from the Devil, the whole bunch of 'em."

"I heard it was the Devil took that Injun's tongue."

I wanted to say it *was* a devil who took Ezra's tongue, a savage devil named Weasel. I wanted to say that Ezra was more human than Weasel and plenty of other folks I could point to. But I didn't. Instead I asked, "Where were they headed?"

"South and east toward Vestry," someone said.

"And after that, to Milltown."

"You should be able to catch 'em in a day or two or three. They move slow with them wagons, and they might spend two, three days at the same place, long as folks keep coming."

I'd found Ezra's trail at last.

10

TIME CRAWLED ALONG slow as a centipede for the next three days, as we traveled to Vestry. Every minute we spent there was an agony to me. While Beckwith peddled his wares, the townsfolk talked about how the show had packed up and left just the day before for Milltown, after staying for two nights' worth of performances.

They marveled at how skinny the human skeleton feller was, and how teeny Little Miss Mary was, and how big the Amazing Amelia was for her age. But what they talked about most was "that wretched soul," the White Injun who had no tongue. One man said it showed what savages Injuns were.

Beckwith and I moved on, and I had lots of time to think as we made our way eastward. I thought about Weasel and how he was as close to pure evil as a man could be, and more savage than any Indian I'd ever heard of.

Orrin Beckwith was a puzzle. He talked about a man being either a wolf or a sheep, but I didn't think it was that simple when it came to most folks. Why, Beckwith himself had a way of being a wolf one minute and a sheep the next. Besides, even wolf mothers suckled their young, and sheep sometimes trampled one another to death when they got to running scared. Thinking about it near wore me out.

When Beckwith and I finally dragged our sorry, tired selves to the outskirts of Milltown, we saw a handbill on a tree just like the one I'd been carrying in my pack ever since we left home. I'd been pushing Beckwith hard, and we hadn't stopped to rest much the past few days, or to wash up the way we usually tried to do. I reckon we didn't look like much, but what did I care? I was close to Ezra. Soon he and I'd be on our way back to Pa and Molly and the harvest.

"You're twitchy as a sack of wet cats," Beckwith complained. "You go on to town and find your friend and I'll set up camp here by the river. Then I aim to have me a bath." He eyed me. "Some would say you should do the same."

"I will," I said. "Soon as I've got Ezra."

That afternoon a lady had paid for her ribbons and comb with fresh-made biscuits and butter, a pot of jam, and some bacon.

"I earned that food, too, by fiddling," I reminded Beckwith. "So make sure it doesn't disappear down your gullet before Ezra and I get back."

Beckwith and I had fallen into the habit of trading insults back and forth, the way he had with Honeywell.
But he didn't offer a smart answer this time. He only
gave me a nod and a peculiar look. I figured he was
wanting to say something, but biting on his tongue
not to.

I left my pack behind at camp, but made sure I was
wearing both Ezra's black hat and the locket he'd given
to Molly, so he'd see them right off. I pictured his face
lighting up when he saw me, and the way his ears wiggled when he smiled real big, and I nearly laughed out
loud.

I made sure my gold piece was way down in my boot
and my knife hung at my side. I was ready.

Farther along the river and closer to town, I came
upon a couple of horses, hobbled so they wouldn't range
off too far, munching on the thick grass. Soon I could see
three show wagons set in a half circle by the river. They
had canvas sides rigged on 'em, so I couldn't see inside.
There was lettering on the canvas saying pretty much the
same things as the handbill, except that the names of
the owners of the outfit were added: Hiram and Lovey
Trask.

Between the wagons and the river was a clearing. A
fire with a big pot hanging over it sent up a lazy twist of
smoke. Clothes and a couple of blankets were drying on
a rope tied between two trees.

At first I didn't see anybody, but then I heard a high-
pitched giggle and looked around. Two people sat on the

back of one of the wagons, their legs hanging down. Two of the legs hung low and two dangled short. As I approached, it didn't take me long to figure I had to be looking at Calvin Edson, the Human Skeleton, and Little Miss Mary. Edson wasn't only the skinniest man I'd ever seen, but also the tallest. And Little Miss Mary was just what the handbill had said, a grown lady only two feet tall.

It was Little Miss Mary who was doing the giggling.

"Hey, there!" she called to me. "You can't come looking around here any time you want. You have to pay good money to see monstrosities like us!" She poked the man next to her with an elbow, kicked her short legs, and gave a hoot of laughter. Then she took a long swig from a bottle she held in her hand.

"Don't let her scare you off," said the skinny man I'd figured was Edson. "Little Miss Mary's been tippling, and it always makes her a bit . . ." He paused, thinking.

Little Miss Mary piped up, "Ornery?"

"No, I was about to say *feisty*," answered Edson. "Or perhaps *outspoken*. Never would I call such a lovely lady as you *ornery*."

"Why, thank you, Calvin. May I say it's a pleasure to pass the time of day with a true gentleman such as yourself." She giggled again and moved her eyelashes up and down at Edson. "Seeing as we're so suited to each other, how about we get married? The Trasks could charge admission to the ceremony. What a 'curiosity' that would be! And our children! Why, Lovey and Hiram could make a bundle. What do you say, Calvin, shall you and I get married?"

Little Miss Mary enjoyed her joke so much she fell into a laughing fit, and Calvin Edson had to pat her back to keep her from choking. When she'd recovered herself, she looked me over and said, "So, young man. Did you come searching for a job? World's Dirtiest Boy, perhaps? I'm afraid the position of wild savage is already taken."

She stared at me and waited for my answer. I'd never heard a voice quite like hers. It was pitched high, the same as her laugh, and sounded *little*, somehow, like the rest of her. I didn't quite know how to take her. Truth to tell, I found her frightening, though I couldn't have said just why. She was laughing fit to die, but she seemed angry about something, instead of happy, which made me wonder if she was in her right mind.

I didn't have time to think about it just then. "I—I'm looking for somebody," I said. "A friend. I think he might be the savage you're talking about. The one you call the White Injun. Is he here?"

Calvin Edson and Little Miss Mary stared at me like maybe *I* was on display in a show.

"You say you're his friend?" Calvin Edson asked after a minute had gone by with them both looking at me, their eyes and mouths wide open.

"Yes," I said.

Miss Mary and Edson glanced at each other, and I

could have sworn something passed between them, though I was puzzled as to what it might be.

I tried again. "Is he here?" I asked.

"You say you're looking for the White Injun?" Edson said slowly.

"It's what you folks call him, anyhow," I said. "His real name's Ezra Ketcham, and he ain't an Indian or a savage, either."

"You'll have to talk to the Trasks," Miss Mary said. Her lips were set in a straight line. She appeared to have sobered up right quick.

"They're the folks who own the show?" I asked.

"That's their wagon," she said, pointing. "And listen here. Don't tell them you talked to us, understand?"

I shrugged. "Sure," I agreed. "If you say so." I started to walk away. Then I turned back and said, "Ezra—he *is* here, right?"

"Ask the Trasks," said Miss Mary. She was hopping down off the back of the wagon as she spoke, which was a pretty far ways for someone as little as she was. Edson put his feet down and stood up, and they both hurried off and disappeared behind one of the other wagons. It struck me as mighty peculiar behavior.

There didn't seem to be anything to do but find the Trasks. I headed toward the wagon Miss Mary had pointed out, and heard voices coming from inside. I wasn't exactly trying to listen in on somebody else's talk, but I couldn't help it.

"Soon as we get back to South Carolina for the winter,

I say we buy us a new act, something folks out here can't even imagine. If we could find one as good as the Injun, we could get rid of some of the others."

There was some mumbling I couldn't understand, then the same voice, which sounded like a woman's, answered back.

"By next season, or the next, people will be tired of fat ladies, skinny men, and midgets. We need something that'll make people come to us from miles around."

The other mumbly voice asked a question, sounding irritated.

"What, have you gone dim-witted? Why, Amelia alone is eating up half our take every night. We get rid of her and some of the others, we've got fewer mouths to feed. Less expense, more profit."

I was real interested and wanted to listen more, but I was getting nervous. What if they looked out and saw me, or threw open the wagon flaps sudden-like and found me there? I decided I needed to speak up and state my business, especially since it appeared they planned to head off as far as South Carolina.

I cleared my throat real loud and said, "Pardon. I'm sorry to disturb you, but I'm looking for Mr. and Mrs. Trask."

The wagon's canvas door flew open, and a woman peered out. She looked at me narrow-eyed and suspicious. "Who are you?" she asked. "And how long you been standing there? Don't you know better than to sneak up on folks?"

I took off my hat and held it in my hand. "Hello, ma'am. My name is Nathan Fowler and I wasn't sneaking, only wanting to talk to you."

When she kept scowling at me without speaking, I hurried on. "I mean to say I wanted to talk to Mrs. Trask. And Mr. Trask, too."

I stopped as a rifle barrel appeared, followed by another face, this one a man's. He didn't speak, either, just stared at me like I smelled bad. Maybe I did, at that, but he hardly seemed close enough to tell. Anyhow, it wasn't what I'd call polite, even though he did lower the rifle after a minute or two.

Finally he said, "I'm Trask. We're not hiring, if it's a job you want."

"No, sir. I'm not looking for work. I got a farm to get back to. A friend of mine is part of your show here, and I came to get him and take him home with me. His name's Ezra Ketcham."

The woman, who I figured for Mrs. Trask, said, "There's no one here by that name."

"Well, I reckon he didn't give his name, seein' as he doesn't talk and he's shy of folks for the most part. But he's the one you call the White Injun," I said, pointing to the side of the wagon with the writing on it.

Mrs. Trask let out a little gasp, and Mr. Trask glared at me hard. Then Mrs. Trask spoke again. "You say you're a friend, not kin, is that right?"

I nodded. I was about to add that the only kinfolk of

Ezra's I knew about had been killed by Weasel, but something stopped me. I wasn't going to tell them Ezra's business when they hadn't told me a darn thing so far.

"Where is he?" I asked. "I'd sure like to see him."

"Well, dearie," began Mrs. Trask, "I'm afraid that won't be possible."

All of a sudden she was smiling and her voice had changed, too. It had a tone to it I recognized, though it took me a minute to figure where I'd heard its like before. It was the way Beckwith talked when he was trying to sell something to somebody.

"Why ever not, Mrs. Trask?" I asked.

"You call me Lovey, now, won't you?" she said, again with that smile that didn't reach her eyes. "And this here's Hiram."

I didn't say anything to that, not being accustomed to calling grown ladies by their first names. Lovey didn't strike me as a proper name, anyway, and it surely didn't suit the hard edges and sharp eyes of Mrs. Trask.

"You see, Mr. Ketcham has left us. We're good friends of his, too," she went on, "so when we saw an opportunity for him to rise in the world, we encouraged him to take it. As I said to Hiram, we could probably have talked Ezra into staying with us, but we knew he could make a lot more money if he traveled to the big cities with that other outfit. We didn't want to hold him back, the poor dear. His life has been so unfortunate, how could we deny him the chance to better himself?"

She paused, appearing quite pleased with herself, and looked from me to Mr. Trask and back. Mr. Trask, who was also smiling now, nodded.

"You mean he's not here?" I asked dumbly, not quite taking in what I was hearing. I tried to remember exactly what I'd overheard them saying. There'd been something about "the Injun," I was sure.

"Not anymore, dearie," said Mrs. Trask, pulling a mournful face. "We did what was best for him, with no thought at all for ourselves. He was our biggest draw, you see. It wasn't easy for us to let him go, you can believe that." She sighed, and gave a little shrug.

But the thing was, I *didn't* believe her. Ezra was there, I knew it. I could feel it. Was I reading Lovey Trask right? I thought I was. So I said, "But I've come from Vestry and he was with you then. That was just three days back."

"Oh, yes, indeed, he was still with us then," she said. The sharp look had come back to her eyes. "But, you see, it was in Vestry that the other show folks saw your friend and made their offer. So we parted ways there, wishing him Godspeed and good fortune. And here we are, without our main attraction, but happy in the knowledge that Ezra is headed for bigger and better things."

"Perhaps," Hiram Trask added, "if you left right away, you could catch up to them. They were going northeast toward Boston, I believe."

"I reckon I'll do that," I said. "Northeast, you say?" I

pretended I was thinking it over. "Yes, I believe I'll try and catch up. Thank you kindly for the information, Mr. and Mrs. Trask."

"Oh, shush, it was nothing," said Mrs. Trask. "And it's Lovey and Hiram, remember? Any friend of Ezra Ketcham's is a friend to us. Do give him our best, won't you? We thought of him as family, Hiram and I did."

I started to go, then turned back like I'd just thought of something. "Too bad I'll be on the road tonight," I said. "I'd have liked to see the show. What time does it begin anyhow?"

"Eight o'clock," said Hiram. "But you'll be well on your way by then, I imagine."

"I reckon so," I said. "I aim to go a good distance before nightfall."

"Safe travels, dearie!" called Lovey.

"I thank you!" I called back.

Beckwith had told me I wasn't a good liar, and maybe I wasn't. I'd have to have a lot of practice to be as good at it as the Trasks. But I figured I'd done all right.

11

MY HEAD WAS BOILING like a tub on washday as I ran back to where Beckwith had set up camp. I was near as mad as I'd ever been in my life. It had taken every bit of my will to hold back from running to the other wagons and searching them till I found where they were keeping Ezra.

I'd stopped myself, and it wasn't only 'cause of Hiram's rifle. I aimed to get Ezra free of the Trasks, and I needed to think out a plan. Already one was starting to take shape in my mind.

Beckwith was washed and dressed and slicking back his hair with a comb when I showed up. Like the show folks, he had a line hung up with some clothes airing, and a fire going. I poured out the whole story of what I'd seen and heard.

"So I figure we'll go back there tonight, when the Trasks will have Ezra out in plain sight for the show," I went on. "They can't say he ain't there in front of all the other folks who'll be looking right at him. And, anyhow, soon as he sees me, that'll be the end of it."

"Those Trasks stated clear that he wasn't there," Beckwith said. "What makes you so sure he is?"

"If you'd been there, you'd have known those Trasks were lying. They only want Ezra to stay so's he can make more money for them. It was plain as the nose on your face!"

Beckwith's expression grew troubled. "Well, if all that's so, what makes you think they're going to let you just walk away with him?"

"I reckon they have to let a free man do what he wants," I said.

"Maybe so," Beckwith said. "But what about that rifle you had pointed in your face?"

"They're not going to shoot me in front of a bunch of people who came to see the show. Besides which, you'll be there, too, as a—a what do you call it?"

"A witness?" Beckwith said uneasily.

"That's it! They won't dare to pull any funny business. Then we'll head on out of there with Ezra."

In my mind the whole thing had already happened, just the way I'd described it. I was so happy imagining Ezra heading with me toward home I guess I didn't notice right at first that Beckwith was backing away from me like I had the pox.

"There ain't no *we* about it, Nathan," he said in a flat

voice. "You've got the wrong fellow. I never signed on to be a witness, or a hero, or to be mixed up in this White Injun affair at all."

I stared at him as he held up his hands, palms out, almost like he was pushing me away.

"I'm just a businessman trying to make my way through this world, Nathan, and get me a stake of money. I don't need any riled-up, rifle-toting showman chasing after me. So you go on. And don't come running back here if you get yourself in a pickle tonight." He paused, then added, "I told your pa I'd help you find your friend, and I did, didn't I? So here's where you and I part company. I hope you got no hard feelings about it."

I shouldn't have been surprised, or disappointed, either. And after a minute or two, I wasn't. Beckwith was only stating the truth of how it was. I was beginning to see that here in the wide world outside our farm, money was real important. To some folks, like Beckwith and Trask, it seemed more important than just about anything.

I shouldered my pack. "I hope you get your stake," I said. "And don't worry. I won't be back, whether Trask's on my tail or not."

"I thank you for that," Beckwith said. "Now, you hold on to what's left of that half eagle." He gave me his foxy grin and added, "When I get out to your place next time, I'll sell your father them spectacles and get it back. Don't you worry. I'll give him a good price."

I might have laughed if I hadn't been thinking so hard on Ezra. "Well, I reckon I'll see you come spring," I said.

"You will," he answered. Then he added, "Unless I make my fortune by then, in which event I'll put down this confounded pack for good and never lift anything heavier than a crystal goblet."

I had to smile at that picture. And, strange as it seemed, I was glad to think I'd see Beckwith again. He was surely right when he said he was no hero. But he'd never pretended he was, either.

"In the meantime, I wish you safe travels, young Nathan."

He put out his hand, and I shook it. "The same to you," I said. I meant it. Then I turned to leave, my thoughts already moving ahead.

I had a couple of hours before the show began, and I had to decide what to do next. I considered heading to the center of town to ask at a tavern if I could fiddle for a meal. But I decided instead to find a place to sit and settle my mind.

When I discovered an old, overturned hay cart that had been abandoned on the bank of a creek headed to the river, I put my pack underneath. From the look of it, the cart had been there for a while. The wheels had fallen off or been taken by somebody, and the wood was rotted. It was grown over by weeds and vines, and made a nice little hiding place. I leaned against its side and went over and over my plan. I figured that Trask couldn't hurt me as long as plenty of townsfolk were there watching.

The sun got low and I put on my hat. I felt for my knife. Leaving my pack under the cart, where it would be safe and dry, I headed toward the Trasks' wagons. When I drew close enough to see what was going on, I hid in a clump of scrubby brush.

Right away, I saw how the setup for the show would work. Hiram Trask was tying ropes between the wagons and onto nearby trees. Then he hung blankets and sheets of canvas on the ropes so the area between the wagons and the river was closed off from view. People who wanted to watch the show would have to pay before they could step through a flap in the canvas and into the clearing.

It wasn't the way I'd imagined it in my plan, and I had to think fast about what to do. I had what was left of my half eagle, so I had more than enough money to get in. But the Trasks would surely recognize me when they counted out my change.

Folks began to come, gathering outside the half circle of wagons and waiting to be let in. Soon there was a pretty big crowd. Then Hiram Trask swept aside the canvas flap in a gesture so grand you'd have thought President Martin Van Buren himself was about to appear.

"Ladies and gentlemen!" he called. "Step right up for admittance to the strangest collection of human oddities, curiosities, and monstrosities ever assembled in history! Be reminded that this show is only for the stout of heart and strong of stomach! Ten cents will get you in the door. After that, brave ladies and gentlemen, you are on your own. Step up now, and have your money ready!"

There was a general commotion as everybody moved

forward together, hoping to get to the front of the line. To my dismay, Lovey Trask joined her husband at the entrance, and they began taking folks' money. I'd never get past both of them.

When everybody was inside, Lovey Trask stayed by the doorway, her eyes darting back and forth from the lighted area around the wagons into the deepening shadows outside. I thought she looked right at me, though I knew she couldn't see me where I hid.

An idea was forming in my head. The only way to view the goings-on and get to Ezra was to sneak in under the wagon closest to where I crouched in the brush.

I heard Hiram Trask bellow, "The first attraction tonight is an example of Nature at her most peculiar and mystifying. I present to you, for your edification and contemplation, a person female in most characteristics, yet with the mustache and whiskers of a man. Ladies and gentlemen: Bearded Betty!"

Trask's announcement was followed by loud toots from a tin horn, then gasps of amazement and horror from the crowd. Lovey Trask turned her head to look inside. Before I could think too much about it, I scurried across the open area, flopped onto my belly, and, stealthy as a wildcat, crawled under the nearest wagon. My hat hit the underparts and fell off my head. I lay still between the wheels, my heartbeats pounding in my ears, waiting. Would there be an outcry from someone who'd heard or spotted me? Or would a face—followed by a rifle barrel—appear beneath the wagon bed?

Nothing happened. I could see the shoes and boots of the folks watching, and that was all. Hiram Trask's voice droned on as he invited someone from the crowd to step up and feel Betty's whiskers to prove they were "no trick, but the genuine article."

I reached for my hat. Snakelike, with the hat in one hand, I slithered on my belly to where I hoped to see the action. Between the shifting legs and bodies of the crowd, I was able to catch glimpses of the platform where Betty stood, her mustache and beard dark brown next to her pale skin, straw bonnet, and yellow dress.

I reckon I was staring as much as anybody. Then a young feller who'd climbed up next to her onstage pulled at her chin whiskers. The crowd cheered, but it seemed to me a shabby thing to do.

Next Trask introduced the Amazing Amelia, who he said was just nine years old and weighed over four hundred pounds. "That's as much as two grown men or four grown ladies." Murmurs rose from the crowd as Amelia was revealed, sitting on a chair on the platform.

"Looks like her folks didn't know the difference between raising a daughter and a prize sow!" Trask added.

I could see Amelia's face clearly in the lantern light. She was looking off into the distance, as if imagining herself somewhere far, far away. I felt my heart squeeze tight.

Pea-Head Pete was next. His head was real little, which I reckon was how he got his name. It came to a point on the top. His eyes went every which way, and his big, yellow teeth stuck out nearly straight from his mouth. He laughed and laughed when the crowd cheered him, drooling and acting the fool. He appeared dim-witted, but whether it was for real or just an act I couldn't have said.

I felt peculiar lying there watching. I couldn't take my eyes off the stage, but at the same time what I was seeing made my stomach kind of churn, the way it did when I was about to be sick. I couldn't wait for Ezra to appear, and at the same time I dreaded it.

Calvin Edson was next. He stood with a grave dignity while Trask went on and on about his height, his weight, and the length of his bones. In the glow from the lantern his thin, bony face did have the look of a skeleton about it, but his bright blue eyes flickered with life.

When Little Miss Mary came onstage, she sang a song in her small, odd voice. Then folks called out questions and she gave them sassy answers.

"What's your pa look like?"

"Handsomer than you, mister."

"How about your ma?"

"Almost pretty as me, only not so delicate-boned."

"You got a husband?"

"You askin' for the job?"

"Sure he is!" someone called.

"Pshaw!" said Little Miss Mary. "He isn't half man enough for a woman like me."

The folks hooted with laughter, clearly loving every minute. Little Miss Mary laughed, too, which puzzled me some. I was sure it was anger, not merriment, I saw burning in her eyes. I could hear it in her voice, even as she smiled and sassed. It made my skin feel prickly, and I was glad when she left the stage.

Then Trask started in hollering about what was coming up next. "We have saved for last, ladies and gentlemen, the most horrifying spectacle of the show, the man known to us as the White Injun!"

In just a moment, I would see Ezra! I wriggled even closer to the edge of my hiding place.

"This would be the time for ladies and children of delicate constitutions to make their departure," Trask went on. "For once you have seen this vision of savagery, you'll never be able to banish the sight from your mind!" He paused for a moment and surveyed the crowd. No one moved.

"You've been warned, my friends. What you are about to see is a white man, but do not make the mistake of thinking he is like you or me. No, sir! For this man was stolen from his family at a young age and raised by savage Injuns, and a man raised by brutal savages cannot be other than a beast himself."

So far, Trask's story was lies, but all I could think of was that Ezra was about to appear. My yearning to see him, to get him away from here and take him home, was so strong I felt my whole body shaking.

The tin horn blew, and Trask said, "When he was first taken as a young child, he begged in his native tongue to be set free to return to his rightful kinfolk, as any poor kidnapped child would do. But his bestial captors could not bear the sound of a civilized voice in their midst. And so they exacted a terrible price, ladies and gentlemen, which you will now witness with your own eyes!"

There was a long silence. Then a figure came shuffling onto the platform, his shoulders drooping and his head hanging low. For a moment I thought this pitiful creature wasn't Ezra, after all. Ezra's posture was upright, and his gait was quick and light. This man appeared weak and frail, where Ezra was healthy and strong.

Then I saw that the man's feet were shackled at the ankles. From my sideways view, I could see that his hands were tied behind his back. From there I could also see Lovey Trask as she came up behind the platform where he stood.

"Look closely, and you will see what the savages did to him when he spoke the language of God and the Bible," Trask shouted.

Lovey Trask drew out a thin leather strap and snapped it quickly, whipping the back of the man's legs. His head came up to face the audience, and his mouth opened wide. I saw his face and knew right off that it was Ezra, even without looking into the gaping black hole of his mouth where his tongue should have been.

Gasps and moans of horror filled the night. I couldn't stand it anymore. I wriggled out from under the wagon, stood up, and began pushing and shoving my way toward the platform.

People shouted angrily as I elbowed past them, but I

didn't care. I reached the show area and faced the platform where Ezra stood.

"Ezra!" I cried. "Ezra! It's me, Nathan!"

His eyes stared straight ahead, and never moved.

"Ezra Ketcham!" I cried again. "It's Nathan Fowler! I'm here to take you home!"

I heard Lovey Trask say a swear word and screech, "What's that boy doing here?"

Rough hands grabbed me from behind, but I shook them off. Quickly I put on my hat and pleaded, "Ezra, look at me. I've got the hat you gave me, remember?" Reaching for my throat, I cried, "And look here. I've got Molly's locket, the one you made her. Ezra, I've come to take you back! Get on down from there, and let's go!"

Still he didn't move.

My outburst had caused a commotion. It was Trask who had grabbed me, and now he gave me a little shove. "See here, son," he said loudly, still playing to the crowd. "What's all this? You're ruining the enjoyment of all these fine folks. Get along now. You're confusing the Injun with someone else. It's clear to everyone he doesn't know you."

People joined in, telling me to leave and stop disrupting the show. I took one last despairing look at the platform. The pale, thin figure stood still as a stone. Its eyes were dull and empty. It was Ezra's body, all right. But Ezra wasn't there.

12

DIMLY I HEARD a high-pitched voice rise above the noise and confusion. "Let the show go on, Mr. Trask. I'll take care of this troublemaker. Pea-Head and Calvin, get over here and give a lady a hand."

The crowd cheered and moved aside to let Little Miss Mary step in front of me. She gave me a fierce look and said, "The show's over for you, mister." To Pea-Head and Calvin, she said, "Take his arms and follow me. Make way, folks, and go back to your fun. Make way, coming through."

Miss Mary led us through the throng of curious people, with Pea-Head Pete and Calvin Edson dragging me along behind her. Folks made room for us, pointing and laughing at the spectacle we made.

I heard Trask boom, "I always say, when you've got a big job needs doing, give it to a midget, ladies and gentlemen. Let's hear it for Little Miss Mary and her cohorts!"

The crowd's roar echoed in my ears as we approached

the entrance to the show. Miss Mary spoke loud, so her small voice carried. "Get out, dirty troublesome boy, and take your crazy notions with you. The Injun doesn't know you, that's plain." She shook her finger at me and added, "And don't come back. We've all had a good eyeful of you, and if Mr. Trask sees you again, he's likely to shoot first and ask questions later, understand?"

When I didn't answer, she asked again, louder. "Understand?"

I nodded dully.

"Good," she said. "Now *git*." With a grand sweep of her hand, she flung open the canvas flap. "Turn him loose, boys," she commanded. Pea-Head and Calvin let go of my arms, and I stumbled forward into the sudden darkness beyond the half circle of wagons.

Once I was outside, I was surprised to feel her small hand gripping mine hard. "Listen," she whispered. "We don't have much time. I'll help you get your friend, but you must do exactly as I say."

I stared at her without speaking, my mind all a jumble, and she went on impatiently. "Come back three hours before first light. Sneak in under the middle wagon and tap on the bottom. I'll hear you." Then she gave me a push and called loudly, "And *stay away*, if you know what's good for you!"

She disappeared inside the canvas, and I was alone. My feet began to move, though my brain was too muddled to tell them where to go.

"Well, *he* won't be back!" I heard Little Miss Mary

announce to the crowd. Their cheers swelled, then rose and fell at my back as I made my way in a daze through the unfamiliar countryside. Slowly my eyes grew accustomed to the night, and I was thankful for the three-quarter moon that had risen.

Somehow I found the overturned cart where I'd left my pack and I crawled under it. I don't know how long I sat curled up there, shaking and sobbing and trying to make sense of what I'd seen and heard. I had imagined finding Ezra over and over in my daydreams, but never had I thought it would happen like this.

There was nobody I could ask, nobody to tell me where Ezra had gone and who the ghost was that had taken his place.

I remembered something Pa had told me when we buried Mama. I'd been crying then, too, and Pa said that even though Mama's body was in the ground, the important part of her, the part that made her Mama, was in heaven.

It seemed the part of Ezra that made him Ezra was gone, too, even though his body wasn't dead and buried. It scared me to think about it.

My poison ivy was gone by then but, still, it looked like that old saying about itchy feet was right. My right foot had sure started me on a long journey. And my left foot had led me to where I wasn't wanted, not even by Ezra.

Some long time later, I made myself sit up straight. Little Miss Mary's words ran through my head over and over. *I'll help you,* she had said. I almost wondered if I'd dreamed it. Why in the world should I believe her, after she threw me out? Why would she help me? She didn't even know me.

It had to be a trick. But for what purpose? So the Trasks could take me prisoner and put me in their show as the World's Stupidest Boy? That's surely what I'd have to be to go back there, risking Trask and his rifle again.

But I had to go back. I couldn't leave Ezra behind after coming so far to find him.

The longer I thought about it, the more I began to believe that Little Miss Mary had been putting on a show of her own to fool the Trasks. For a brief moment outside the light from the wagons, I'd been able to see her eyes. They'd looked right into mine, and again I'd seen the anger in them. I knew somehow it wasn't for me. She was no friend to Trask and that crowd.

I trusted Miss Mary's anger. And I had to trust my own self to be right about what I'd seen.

13

WHEN I COULDN'T STAND waiting anymore, I dragged myself from my hiding place. It took a while to work the pins and needles from my legs and the cramps from my back. The moon had shifted over toward the east, so I figured it was close enough to the hour Miss Mary had told me to return.

With the lanterns unlit and the fire died down, the wagon camp was dark except for the moonlight. That suited me fine. I stood on the outskirts for what seemed the longest time, listening and watching. There were no signs of life other than the hoot of an owl, which always made me feel mournful, and the sounds of small creatures going about their nighttime business. I was grateful for the never-ending murmur and splash of the river, which would help to cover any little noises I made.

There was no reason to wait any longer. If Little Miss Mary had double-crossed me and told the Trasks I was coming, my goose was cooked good. I figured I might as well find out sooner rather than later.

I crept toward the middle wagon. When I sneaked up earlier, my heart had felt ready to burst, but now it thumped steady and calm in my chest. It was strange, I reckoned. But I'd cast my lot with Miss Mary, and now I had to see where it would lead me.

I froze mid-step when I heard a sudden snort from the wagon I knew to be the Trasks'. It was followed by a sigh and the shifting of bodies and rustle of bedding, then by the sound of deep, even snoring. I inched forward again until I was under the middle-wagon bed. After pausing to listen once more, I tapped as lightly as I could on the boards.

So faint I wasn't sure at first it was real, a light tap came back. Then there was the sound of movement, followed by two short legs dangling before my eyes. Little Miss Mary landed on the ground light as a bird and bent down so we were nearly eye to eye.

"Well, dirty boy, here you are," she whispered. She sounded triumphant. "Calvin bet me two bits you wouldn't show. Now he'll have to pay up."

"What about the Trasks?" I whispered back nervously.

She gave a low snort of her own. "I don't reckon anything short of an Indian raid is going to wake those two till well after sunrise. I poured my own good whiskey down their ungrateful throats, making like we were celebrating getting rid of you and keeping the savage in the show." Her eyes glinted in the moonlight. "Well, aren't you going to thank me?"

I was taken aback some by her manner. "Th-thank you," I said.

"Not everyone was in favor of helping you," she whispered. "Amelia is scared to death of Trask, and who can blame her? If he finds out we were in on this, it'll go badly for us. I promised the others I'd handle him, but we've got to tread careful."

She put her fingers to her lips and beckoned to me to come out from under the wagon. I followed her to the next wagon, away from where the Trasks lay sleeping. When I looked up, I saw Calvin Edson's and Pea-Head Pete's anxious faces peering out.

"This here's the men's wagon," Little Miss Mary explained. "What you were under is the women's."

I glanced back and saw that Bearded Betty and the Amazing Amelia were awake, too, and watching us closely. I could see the fear on Amelia's face.

"Ezra's in there?" I asked, gazing at the men's wagon. It was all I could do not to sweep aside the canvas so I could see him.

Little Miss Mary didn't answer right away. In the silence I felt the eyes of all the show people on me. It made me feel prickly, and I wondered uneasily if they might be planning a trick, after all.

"First, hear me out," she said. "After, you may change your mind."

"I won't—" I began, but she shushed me.

"You listen now. I got to know: what do you aim to do with the savage once you have him?"

"His name is Ezra," I said.

Her shrewd expression seemed to grow softer for a moment. "Ezra, then," she said.

"I aim to take him back home with me to our farm."

"And then what?" she asked.

"Well, I don't rightly know," I said uncertainly. "He can do whatever he likes, I reckon, but me and Molly and Pa'd be glad to have him as long as he wants to stay."

She took that in, then asked, "You say you knew him before. Could he speak?"

I shifted uncomfortably from one foot to the other. "Can't I just see him?" I asked.

"In a minute," she said.

I sighed and said, "He couldn't talk then, either. It's a—a long story, how he lost his tongue."

"There's no time for that now," Miss Mary said. "But tell me this, did he have some life about him back then?"

I nodded. "He didn't talk, but he didn't have to. We had a way of getting on together."

"So, besides not talking, he was like other folks?" Miss Mary asked.

It was a difficult question, and it took me a while to sort out the answer. Meantime, I could still feel the eyes of all the other show people, as they leaned forward to hear every word. I wondered if Ezra, inside the men's wagon, was listening, too.

"No, I reckon he was always different, even back then." I blurted out the questions that were tormenting me. "What *happened* to him? Why didn't he even look at me when I called his name?"

I stopped, feeling near to tears.

A loud groan came from the Trasks' wagon, followed by mumbling. I nearly bolted at that, but Miss Mary held my arm and said, "That's just the whiskey talking."

She sighed then. "As to your question," she said quietly, "I don't know. We were out in western Ohio someplace, I remember. Trask went to town and came back with this white feller dressed in tatters and animal skins, wearing his hair long like an Indian." She made a face and added, "Hiram's got a nose for sniffing out misfits and misfortunates."

After another sigh, she went on. "You heard him for yourself: Trask's a cunning liar. I don't know what he said to get your friend to follow him, but I don't suppose it took much. Ezra was mighty dispirited, even then. That very night, Hiram and Lovey put him up on the stage and told their hokum story, made him open his mouth and show the crowd that gaping hole." She paused. "And ever since, I've watched him die a little more every day."

Gesturing with her small hand to the men's and women's wagons, she said, "You see, Calvin, Pea-Head, Betty, Amelia, and me, we belong here. We chose to be here—well, all except for Amelia. Her parents sold her to the Trasks when she was just six years old."

I shook my head in wonder at such a thing.

"Here we have a roof over our heads, and food, such as it is," Miss Mary said. "I know that doesn't sound like much, and maybe it isn't. But we also have each other's company. Out in the world, people stare and say cruel things. Of course, they do that at the show. But they have to pay for the pleasure and, to us, that makes all the difference."

Her keen eyes peered at me in the darkness to see if I was following. I nodded to show I got her meaning well enough. I did, too. But I was so impatient to get to Ezra, it was hard to stand and listen.

"Your friend, he doesn't belong here," Miss Mary said. "Trask knows that. I figure that's why he keeps him apart."

"Apart?" I repeated warily. "How do you mean?"

Little Miss Mary hesitated, then took my hand before saying, "The rest of us, we're not allowed to talk to him. Trask keeps him alone, in that—that *cage*." She pointed with her other hand.

"*Cage!*" I gasped. I broke free of her grasp and ran past the end of the men's wagon to where a boxlike shape stood half-hidden in the brushy undergrowth near the riverbank. It wasn't much more than some boards nailed to a frame, with some hinges to allow for a door, and a canvas thrown over the top. I'd seen chicken coops and corncribs built better. It filled me with horror to think that this was where Trask kept Ezra. But I was confused, too. There wasn't any lock on the door, so what was keeping Ezra there?

"Ezra?" I whispered finally. There was no answer.

Miss Mary appeared at my side again. Quietly she said, "Trask used to lock him in. He stopped when he saw that your friend didn't even try to get away."

With a feeling of dread, I pulled the door open. I did it slowly, not knowing if the hinges might need oiling, and was grateful when they didn't make a sound. At first it was hard to make out anything in that dark, cramped space. But then the moonlight shone in on a figure lying slumped against the wall. I stepped in, bent down, and took Ezra by the shoulders.

"Come on, Ezra," I whispered urgently. "We're getting out of here."

His eyes opened, but there was no sign that he recognized me or even cared who I was. He closed his eyes, and his head rolled onto his chest. Altogether he put me in mind of a doll Molly had when she was a baby, made out of raggedy old clothes. I shook Ezra gently, and heard the clanking sound of metal.

The shackles! He was still wearing them. I turned to Miss Mary in despair.

"Trask clamped those things on that first day. Calvin and me, we talked about trying to get 'em off tonight, but we couldn't take the risk."

I put my head in my hands. It was all too much.

"Those shackles, there's not a lot to 'em, really," Miss

Mary said. "They're mostly for show, to convince the crowd how dangerous the savage is." She snorted with contempt at the idea. "Calvin and me, we think you might get 'em off pretty easy. You got any tools?"

I pointed to my Barlow hanging at my side, and she looked at it doubtfully. "Nobody here would blame you if you backed out and went on home," she said.

I felt too hopeless to speak.

Little Miss Mary continued, "But, like I said, Calvin and me talked it over a good bit. We thought of a way you just might do this."

I looked at her. "How?"

"Well, your friend here is weak as a newborn kitten from being shackled. He barely eats enough to keep alive. He barely *is* alive, if you see my meaning."

My feelings at that must have shown on my face, because Miss Mary went on quickly. "So you'll need a place to hole up for a while. Someplace Trask won't find you if he comes looking, and I expect he will. Someplace close, 'cause you won't get far with him the way he is, even if he wasn't shackled."

"I got a place," I said. "But I don't know if I can get him there. It's—"

She held out her hand to stop me. "Shhh. Don't tell me. If Trask suspects you had help, the less we know, the better."

I could see the sense in what she said, and I tried to calm myself and listen.

"Once you get to your hide, you stay there for a while. Three, four days, however long it takes for him to get his strength up," she was saying. "It'll give you time to figure a way to get those shackles off. Assuming Trask doesn't find you in the meantime, of course," she added.

"We'd best get started," I said.

She nodded. "I wanted to be sure you knew what you were getting into," she said. Then she handed me a sack. "This here's food."

She signaled to Pea-Head and Calvin, and they came over and helped me get Ezra to his feet. He didn't raise his head, or twitch a limb. A quivery feeling, like hundreds of little fish were swimming through my insides, rose up in me. It made me feel weak, and I tried to fight it down.

I'd been real scared before in my life, when I'd been stalked like an animal through the forest by the killer called Weasel. But I'd never felt so afraid as I did right then. Looking into the emptiness of Ezra's face frightened me so bad I wanted to run and not stop till I got home to the farm.

Miss Mary was staring at me with a concerned expression. "It's not a fit job to ask of a boy," she murmured to the others.

I shook my head. I could do it. I *would* do it. Holding the sack of food in my left hand, I braced myself as Pea-Head and Calvin draped Ezra's arm over my right shoulder. I grasped him around the waist. He flinched from my touch, like he'd been burned, and grew stiff. It made me sadder than anything that he didn't know me, didn't know I'd never hurt him.

"Come with me now, Ezra," I said, soft and gentle as I could. "It's not far."

We took a few slow, shuffling steps. The chain between Ezra's shackled ankles clanked faintly. The rustle of old, dead leaves beneath our feet seemed louder, somehow, filling each step with fear of waking the Trasks.

Miss Mary walked alongside us, looking scared and worried, too.

"Thanks to you, Miss Mary," I whispered. "To all of you. I wish—"

She broke in and said, "You just get home safe, you hear?"

I swallowed hard. "I will." I looked back and saw Calvin, Pea-Head, Betty, and Amelia watching us, their faces full of fear and hope.

"I will," I said again, trying to sound like I was sure, and wishing I could be.

Ezra and I made our slow and painful way through the night. I didn't dare look back, or think ahead any farther than the next step.

14

THE SUN WAS GIVING off a pale light and I was more exhausted than I'd ever been by the time Ezra and I made it to the overturned cart. I don't recollect much about getting there, other than being glad for every step we made without falling or getting caught by Trask.

Somehow I pushed and rolled Ezra underneath and crawled in behind him. Then I thought to get water from the creek for what would likely be a long day hiding in that small, closed space. I worried what Ezra might do while I was gone. But when I got back, he hadn't moved at all, far as I could tell.

I held a cup of water to his mouth, tilted his head back, and poured slowly. In the sack of food from Miss Mary I found biscuits, cooked beans wrapped in the big leaves from wild grape vines, some chunks of cooked meat, several apples, and corn bread. I ate an apple, which was good, though sharp-tasting from being picked green. I couldn't get Ezra to eat so much as a bite.

All the time, I was listening for the sound of approaching footsteps. Miss Mary had figured Trask would come after us, and I didn't doubt it was true. If he'd had dogs, we'd have been sunk. Being so close together in that small space, I could tell Ezra hadn't been given the opportunity for a bath in a long while, and I knew I didn't smell so good myself. I had to hope Trask didn't know much about tracking. Pa or just about any Shawnee could have followed our trail quicker'n a fox on a rabbit.

I didn't mean to, but I dropped into sleep. A light rain had begun falling, drumming a rhythm on the boards overhead that lulled me. I dreamed about the night Ezra had led me and Molly through the forest to get to Pa. He'd been so quick and quiet, like a wild creature that could see in the dark. I woke up suddenly, and almost despaired again, wondering what could have happened to change Ezra into this dull, clumsy stranger.

Then I heard voices coming our way, and realized that they must have been what woke me. The loud rustling of several people approaching through the underbrush made my heart jump into my throat. They were very close. Out of instinct or habit, I reckon, I put my finger to my lips in a signal for quiet, but Ezra wasn't watching.

"Even if he got the shackles off, they can't have got far." It was Trask. "Not with that half-wit hardly able to stand hisself upright."

Holding my breath, I moved my head slightly so I could see out through a space between two boards. Pea-Head Pete and Calvin Edson were walking on either side of Trask. They were moving along in a row, looking down at the ground for signs of our trail. Trask's face was red and irritable-looking. He was shading his eyes in a pained way, and I figured maybe he was feeling the effects of all the whiskey he'd drunk the night before. He saw the cart and began heading straight for our hiding place.

I drew my knife, imagining how he'd laugh when he tipped over the cart and knocked it from my hand with the tip of his rifle.

"Boss!" It was Calvin Edson's voice.

Trask was just three or four steps away—close enough, I was sure, to hear the pounding of my heart. "What is it?" he hollered, sounding in a right ill humor.

"Over here," said Edson urgently. "Quick! I think I see footprints."

Trask turned away and headed toward where Calvin stood peering at the ground.

Before I had time to feel relieved, Pea-Head called, "I'll check under that cart for you, boss." Next I heard his footsteps approaching, and I held my breath again. I was glad it wasn't Trask coming, but I didn't know for sure if Pea-Head had good sense. Did he have a grasp on what was happening, or did he maybe think it was all a game, like hide-and-seek?

I was about to find out.

Pea-Head let out a groan as he crouched down to his knees to peer into our hiding place. Through the space between two boards our eyes met, and I felt myself stiffen as he let out a high-pitched giggle. I closed my eyes, waiting for him to call out to Trask that he'd found us.

"Nothin' here but a nest of mice, boss," he yelled.

I opened my eyes, and I could have sworn I saw him wink at me before he stood up and walked away.

Trask called back, "Then go look sharp in the soft mud there by the creek bank, you hear?"

After a moment Pea-Head let out his giggle again and answered, "Looks like raccoons been in the creek, that's all."

"Darn rain made their tracks hard to read, boss," said Calvin. "But I'd say it looks like we should try going this-a-way."

Still crouching like a cornered animal, I remained rigid, listening until there was nothing more to hear. Even then, I didn't dare move for a long time. Thinking about it, I decided Calvin had suspected Ezra and I might be under the cart, and had led Trask off someplace else. Silently I thanked him, hoping he'd taken Trask far away.

I'd been pretty sure Trask would get mean when he woke up and found Ezra gone, and I'd worried that Amelia's fear of Trask would cause her to tell him about the others' helping me. I'd also worried that one of the show folks who had been my allies in the dark of night might feel different come daylight, when faced with Trask's anger. So far it appeared they'd been steadfast, and for that I was thankful.

But now that Trask hadn't found us, his temper would most likely turn even uglier. I thought about moving to a new spot, but I didn't know if there was anything nearby that would serve as well as the cart to hide the two of us. I had to hope that if Trask continued to look for us, he wouldn't head back where he'd already searched once.

If only Ezra were stronger, and not shackled . . . I stopped myself. No sense in wishing for what might be. Better to keep my mind on what was, though it made a dreary picture.

At least one of my worries—that Ezra might give us away—seemed foolish now. He was so still and quiet I found myself looking to see if his chest was rising and falling with breath.

I didn't try to talk to him. I was too afraid of Trask sneaking back to risk making a sound. But, truth to tell, I was glad for a reason not to talk. Ezra had never been able to answer me in words, but his face and body had always been alive with his thoughts, and he'd had a way of acting out what he wanted to say. It was uncanny, Pa used to say.

But talking to someone who didn't give you any kind of answer was lonesome business. It scared me, the way Ezra behaved like I wasn't even there. It made me feel hopeless, and I couldn't let myself get discouraged. We weren't yet free and clear of Trask and we still had a long trip ahead.

I spent my time eyeing and feeling those shackles, thinking how I might get them off. There wasn't much to them, just like Miss Mary had said. A thin band of metal was bent into a circle around each of Ezra's ankles. The ends of the bands overlapped slightly.

From the greenish color they left on his skin, I figured they were copper, and that gave me a glimmer of hope. I knew copper was soft. Well, soft for metal, anyhow. That was the reason Trask had been able to clamp them on. Still, the force of bending them around Ezra's legs must have hurt him something terrible.

A heavy chain hung between the bands. Unlike the bands, it looked and felt to be made of iron. Before Trask bent the bands shut around Ezra's ankles, he must have first slipped the end links of the chain onto them.

The skin on Ezra's ankles was rubbed raw, and the greenish color from the copper only made it look worse. The sight fed my fury at Trask. I forced myself to think instead about how to get Ezra free.

The chain itself would be impossible to cut through without a blacksmith's tools, and I didn't dare march Ezra into a town like Vestry and ask for help in setting him free. There'd be too many questions, and word might get to Trask somehow.

I was going to have to work on the softer copper bands myself. The problem put me in mind of cutting through my half eagle coin. I wished for Orrin Beckwith's little hammer and chisel, though I didn't relish the idea of pounding on the bands with Ezra's ankles inside them.

I figured I'd try to pry the bands open with my knife,

rather than attempting to cut through them. A Barlow is a fine tool, but I didn't know if it was strong enough for what I had in mind.

When the food from Little Miss Mary was gone, I'd need the knife to get more. I reached for some nearby sticks, and passed the time whittling snares for catching rabbits and small ground birds. That way I'd have them, even if my knife broke while I worked on the shackles.

I waited until after dark that night, and when Trask hadn't returned, I crawled out from under the cart into the pale moonlight. I pulled and poked and prodded until I got Ezra to come out, too. Then, to coax him to walk a little, I spoke in a hushed voice. "I'll get those shackles off soon as I can, Ezra. I know it's hard for you to walk with them on. But we need to start getting you strong for traveling."

He didn't seem to take any notice of my words, so I hung on to his arm and we commenced taking small steps, the way we'd done before. We hadn't gone far when a harsh voice tore through the night.

"Stop right there, boy, and put your hands in the air."

I froze like a scurrying nighttime creature that feels the whoosh of the owl's wings overhead just a moment too late.

15

THE VOICE I KNEW to be Trask's came from the shadows again. "You heard me. Or have you gone deaf and dumb like the Injun?"

I let go of Ezra's arm and raised my hands. Peering toward the sound, I saw moonlight glinting off metal. Then I made out Trask, aiming the rifle my way.

"I'm taking the Injun back with me," he said. His flat tone said there wasn't any point in arguing. "I'm tired of you, boy. And when I'm tired, my finger gets jumpy."

My eyes flew to his finger against the trigger.

"There's nobody around here that knows who you are. Nobody that cares. Folks back where you came from ain't got any idea where you are right now. I could kill you, leave you in the woods to rot, and who would know the difference? Or you could turn over the Injun and forget we ever met." He shrugged. "Your choice, boy."

In my mind, I saw his finger tighten on the trigger. I

heard the shot, and saw myself fall to the ground, dead. I saw Trask going off with Ezra, leaving my body to the scavenging animals that would surely come. In the quiet that seemed to go on forever, I saw Pa and Molly waiting and waiting for me to return, and finally, sadly, giving up hope. I saw Ezra, back in the show, no better off than he'd been before, and maybe worse.

I didn't want to die. But I'd come so far to rescue Ezra. I *had* to take him home with me, or everything I'd done had been for nothing.

I couldn't move or speak, just stood with my hands in the air.

Trask let out a loud, impatient sigh. "I'm gonna take the Injun now. Stay where you are."

He moved toward us. Beside me, Ezra stood still as a stone. Trask approached close enough so his sour smell filled my nostrils. "Back to work, chief," he said, grabbing Ezra roughly by the arm and pushing him in the direction of the wagon camp.

Ezra stumbled and nearly fell. Without knowing I was going to do it, I reached out to steady him. With my other hand, I pushed Trask away.

Then I felt the sharp jab of a rifle butt in my side, and fell to the ground in pain.

❁

The night sky seemed to twirl in circles. Dizzily I rolled over, got to my knees, leaned forward, and heaved until my stomach was empty and my mouth was dry. I knelt, gasping, while the world stopped spinning. When the pain in my side allowed me to, I got to my feet.

I shook my head to clear it, and looked around. There was no sign of Trask or Ezra. I listened for the shuffle of their footsteps, but heard nothing except the sound of my own breath, ragged in my throat.

I started in the direction of the wagon camp. I had no plan in my mind, and no thought of what I'd do when I got there. It was simply the only thing I could think to do, though I don't reckon I was really thinking. All I knew was that, right then, the idea of heading back home without Ezra seemed impossible. I wasn't going to crawl back under that cart, either. So I walked.

I did it the way Pa had taught me when we were hunting. I walked a bit, stopped still to listen hard, then walked a little more. I knew Trask couldn't move very fast, not with Ezra beside him, shackled. I'd had the breath knocked out of me, but I hadn't been lying on the ground very long. I believed I'd soon catch up to Trask.

After I'd walked a while and stopped to listen several more times, I heard rustling in the leaves ahead, then a muffled voice, saying something angry and impatient. Trask.

I crept along behind them, thankful for the nearly full moon, being careful not to make a sound. Recalling the knife hanging at my side, I drew it and held it ready. Ready for what, I didn't know.

I was drawing close when I stepped on a branch that snapped under my foot with a sharp crack. Trask, Ezra, and I all froze. Then Trask whirled around, his rifle once again aimed my way. When he saw me, his shoulders slumped and he swore softly.

I'd looked down the muzzle of that rifle more times than I cared for. It seemed Trask was forever pointing it at me. I reckoned I was about to find out if he'd really shoot it. I was scared, but for some reason I also felt strangely calm. I wasn't leaving without Ezra, so it was up to Trask.

The thing was, a little part of my mind kept remembering Beckwith and all his talk of reading folks like books. Thinking back on what I'd seen of Trask, I read him as a liar and a crook. I read him as greedy, and lazy. He was a showman and a faker. But I didn't take him for a cold-blooded killer, like Weasel.

I'd looked deep into Weasel's eyes, and I would never forget what I'd seen there. I should say it was what I *hadn't* seen that chilled me to my bones. There was nothing in those eyes of any human feeling.

But where Weasel was through and through what Beckwith would call a wolf, it struck me that Trask was like most ordinary folks: part wolf and part sheep. That's how I figured him, anyway. Most likely it was foolhardy of me to think so. This business of reading folks was new to me, and there was a good chance I was going about it wrong. But, I told myself, I'd read Miss Mary right when she'd said she would help me.

I was thinking, too, about times when I'd watched the menfolk playing cards at Whitefield's store in town.

Now, after spending time with Beckwith, I understood how they were all trying to read faces to find out how good the other players' cards might be. They put up a lot of bluff and bluster to fool one another. Maybe Trask was doing just that. Maybe I could play the game, too.

"The thing is, Mr. Trask," I said, "I came a long ways to get my friend, and I aim to take him back with me."

Trask stared at me with an odd expression, almost like he couldn't quite believe what he was hearing. But he hadn't shot me yet, so I kept on talking.

"I reckon you can find yourself another act pretty quick, somebody like Little Miss Mary, who knows what's what. Looks to me like keeping Ezra caged and shackled is more trouble than it's worth."

He was listening. That was good. I'd watched Orrin Beckwith when he was trying to make a sale, and he never stopped talking as long as a body was listening. So I went on. "You know he'll die soon if he stays. He's not far from dyin' now. Then what have you got?"

In the bright moonlight, I saw Trask's eyes narrow.

"You've got the worth out of him. You'd be better off to get shed of him now, before he gets too sick to earn his keep."

Trask looked from me to Ezra, like he was sizing up just how much longer Ezra might last.

I played my final card. "I got four dollars in gold to pay you right now if you let him go," I said. It hadn't entered my head to make such an offer before, I reckon because paying money for a human being was a peculiar piece of business. It was being desperate that made me think of it at all.

"I could shoot you, take the Injun *and* the money," Trask growled. "What's to stop me?"

My heart sank. If I'd read him wrong, there was no good answer to his question. We stood, our eyes locked, for what seemed like a very long time.

Then Trask heaved a loud sigh and swore again. He shoved Ezra so hard he fell, and said, "He'll likely croak before you get four dollars' use out of him, and it'll be on your head, not mine."

I didn't make any answer to that. Quick, I took off my boot and dug out the rest of Mama's gold piece. I walked over and, without a word, handed Trask the money.

With difficulty, I pulled Ezra to his feet. Putting one arm around his waist to hold him up, I began leading him away. I felt Trask's eyes on my back as Ezra and I made our way slowly through the trees. I imagined Trask weighing the gold in one hand and the rifle in the other, making his final decision.

Then I heard the sound of his footsteps as he turned at last and walked away.

16

EZRA AND I HID out all the next day. I couldn't believe Trask had given up for good. I about wore myself
out, jumping at every splash of a frog, every chirp from a
bird or chatter from a squirrel. But come evening, there'd
been no sign of Trask.

Warily, I drew Ezra out for water and a walk. We returned to the cart, where I slept badly. In the morning, I
took my knife to the band on Ezra's left leg. I was afraid
that, however gentle I tried to be, I was going to hurt
him when I put force on the metal. So I tucked the edge
of the quilt Molly had given me between the band and
Ezra's ankle.

I explained to him what I was about to do, and how I
hoped not to hurt him, but I couldn't tell if he even heard
me. Then, slowly and real carefully, I worked the blade
between the two ends of the band at the point where
they overlapped each other.

"I'm going to take my time, Ezra, so the knife doesn't slip. If I hurt you, you let me know and I'll stop, all right? Now I'm going to wiggle the knife a little, like this." I wiggled it as I spoke. "I'm going to keep doing it until I get it in there a ways—like that! Now I'll wiggle a little more . . . See? It's going in a bit farther every time."

Holding my hand steady, I kept at it until I got the blade wedged far enough between the two overlapping parts that I could see the tip come out the other side, and I began to use the knife to pry the bands apart. It was working, and I was feeling really excited when suddenly the tip of the blade snapped off. Ezra's ankle jerked away from my grasp and I dropped the knife.

I looked quickly at Ezra's face to see if I'd hurt him, but if he *had* grimaced, I'd missed it. His expression was blank. I picked up the knife to examine it. About a half inch of the tip was gone. It was the sharpest, narrowest part, which meant I was going to have a harder time starting on the second shackle. If I ever got to the second one. I couldn't think about that.

I'd managed to pry the bands apart about a quarter of an inch. As I'd hoped, the metal of the blade was harder than the copper. It had snapped only because I'd twisted it too much right at its thin tip.

I held the knife sideways so I was using the thicker part of the blade to separate the bands enough to almost fit my thumb between them. Sweat was pouring down my face by the time I finished. After a careful look around, I left our shelter and searched out a thin, flat stone. I used the edge to pry the bands farther still, until, finally, the copper gave way and the band slid off.

Through it all, Ezra never moved again, or made a sound. Having the shackle on or off appeared to be all the same to him. But, tired as I was, I was pleased at what I'd done, even though the chain still hung from the band on Ezra's other leg.

I felt bad making him practice walking that night, dragging the chain behind him, but it was a lot easier for him now that his one leg was free. I fell asleep with the first feelings of hope I'd had since leaving the show.

The next day I began work on the second shackle. I got a scare when some folks who were traveling by horse and wagon stopped at the creek for water and a rest. A man, a woman, and a boy younger than Molly came right over and sat by our cart, leaning against its side same as I had done when I first saw it.

I barely breathed for the whole time they were talking and eating, not an arm's length away from where Ezra and I sat. I couldn't even have said what it was they talked about, I was that edgy. They were likely harmless, but I didn't relish explaining why I was hiding out with a man who was half-shackled and half-dead. Much as I wanted Ezra to come back to life, I dearly hoped he wouldn't pick that moment to do it.

Some other folks on horseback came by later, but none was Trask, and they didn't bother us any.

The sun had nearly set when I finished getting the second shackle off. It took a lot longer than the first one, being as my knife tip was gone. By the time I finished, the whole blade was near ruined, but I didn't care. I threw those bands and the chain as far as I could into the forest, hoping never to see their like again.

It was good to watch Ezra walk free that night. We went up and down the creek bank until I thought he'd had all he could take.

Never once in that time did Ezra look at me or change his slack, far-off expression. Surely those days I spent hidden under the cart with his ghost were the longest of my life.

By the fourth day, Ezra would take water if I handed him a cup, though I had to put small bits of food in his mouth to get him to eat. I was feeling sure Trask must have moved on. That night, I let go of Ezra's arm as we walked, and I just went along beside him. When he seemed to be keeping up, I stepped out ahead and picked up my pace, slow at first, then a little faster. He came along behind me, which relieved me some, although it made me sad to see him so tame, following me like a puppy dog.

I'd begun talking to him more and more. I couldn't stand the silence, partly. But I also got to thinking about how Mama always rocked us and sang to us when we were sick, along with giving us the medicines and tonics she made from her roots and herbs.

I remembered, too, when Pa was wild with fever that time back in Ezra's we-gi-wa. Molly had done the same for him. Later, he had told us he reckoned her talking soothed him just as much as the white-root poultice and witch hazel Ezra used to wash and heal the wounds on his leg.

So I talked to Ezra whenever I felt it was safe. He never let on that he understood what I was saying, or heard me at all, for that matter. It made *me* feel better, though, even if he took no notice.

We ate the last of our food that night. Before we slept, I set out a couple of my snares. In the morning, I had caught a rabbit. I waded into the creek where a bunch of little fish swam in the shallows, and trapped them in a corner of my blanket. Then I built a fire, our first, right out in the open. I cooked the rabbit and the fish and wrapped them up for later. And Ezra and I left our hiding place and started for home.

17

WE WALKED SOME that day; rested, walked a little more, rested, and walked again. I headed in a westerly direction, back toward Vestry without going too close to the town, where someone might recognize Ezra and raise a ruckus. When I feared tiring him too much, I stopped and made camp.

"You showed me how to throw your Shawnee hunting stick, remember?" I said as I put a pot on to boil water. I'd found some leaves I knew were good for making a strengthening tea, and some berries to add for sweetness.

"I didn't think that old stick would do me much good, but I threw it at Weasel when he sneaked up on me that night. It hit his rifle and made him shoot his own self in the leg!"

I peered at Ezra over the flames of our fire to see if his face showed anything. Months earlier, when I'd first told him that story, he'd whooped and banged his fist on his knee and laughed so hard tears had rolled down his cheeks. This time he only stared into the fire.

I didn't stop talking, though. I thought I'd try asking questions. Maybe that would make him want to answer. "Where'd you go after you left us, Ezra?" I paused, and when there was no answer, I went on talking. "We wondered and wondered about you, and made up all kinds of stories about what you were doing."

After a moment of silence, I tried another subject. "I thank you for leaving me your hat, Ezra. You left it in the stone wall outside our cabin, remember? I wear it most all the time. I never got to thank you proper. And Molly gave me this to show you." I pulled out the bone locket from under my shirt. "She'll want it back soon as we get home. It's her favorite thing in the world, along with Mama's medicine bag and those blue beads you gave her."

His eyes didn't so much as flicker.

"When you went off, Molly was so happy to think you weren't going to be alone anymore. She was hoping you'd get married again."

He didn't show any signs of hearing me. Maybe that's why I went ahead and said something I'd been keeping quiet about. "I reckon Pa's thinking about getting married to Miss Abigail Baldwin."

I didn't expect him to answer, but I went on as if he'd stated an opinion. "So you think it's a good idea? Well, Molly does, too. She says Mama wouldn't want Pa to be lonesome, and I expect she's right. It'd be nice for Molly to have the company. And Pa, too, of course. I believe Pa's waiting on me to speak up, one way or the other." I shrugged. "I've been thinking about it some, and I reckon it might be all right."

I peered at him, but his expression hadn't changed. I tried another subject.

"I got me a fiddle, Ezra. I told you I would someday, remember? I went to see Eli, and he gave me lessons."

I took the fiddle out of my pack, unwrapped the quilt, and touched the smooth, shiny wood. I'd missed being able to play it while we were hiding.

"Feel that," I said, and I got up and walked around so I could put the fiddle in Ezra's lap. I took his hand and ran it along the curved side of the instrument. "Isn't that something? I think it's about the most beautiful thing I ever saw."

I went back and sat down to tune it. Whenever I tuned up at home, Molly said it was like wildcats screeching, but Ezra didn't blink an eye.

"I don't reckon I'm any good yet," I went on. "But Eli says I will be one day, if I work hard. He says I've got a good ear. What do you say to that?"

I began with the tunes I knew, the ones I'd played to draw customers for Beckwith. I played until I was plumb wore out from it, and even then I kept on going.

Finally I put the fiddle away, saying, "That's all for now, Ezra. We got to get some sleep. But I'll play again in the morning, and every night and every morning till we get home, I promise. I reckon if you get tired of it, you'll just have to let me know."

We spent the next few days traveling, and I could see Ezra growing stronger every day. I didn't have to force him to eat anymore. I reckon he got hungry from walking, same as I did. But I told myself it also meant he cared whether he lived or died, and I took that as a good sign.

On the trip east with Beckwith, I'd paid close attention to the rivers we'd crossed and the terrain we'd passed through. I knew to use the sun to travel nearly straight west till we reached the river the Shawnees called the Big Turkey and we called the Ohio. Then I'd shift northwest to the country where our farm was.

I avoided the towns, unlike when I'd traveled with Beckwith. The less we saw of civilization, the better off we were, as I figured it. Ezra had always been wary of folks, even before Trask got hold of him. Now he reminded me even more of a wild creature, and I tried to gentle him same as I would any one of 'em that needed it.

I'd taken to touching Ezra in small ways, patting his shoulder when I handed him his food, or putting my hand on his when I said good night. He didn't flinch from me anymore, and I didn't want any strangers scaring him off.

I played my fiddle for him each morning and evening,

and I got to thinking he looked forward to it. One night, when we'd finished eating from a pot of squirrel stew I'd fixed, I'd taken out my fiddle and commenced tuning.

A voice from the forest said, "I hope you're working up to playing a tune, Nathan Fowler, because that racket surely isn't what's commonly known as *music*."

Out of the shadows stepped Joseph R. Honeywell, his dandylion hair standing out from his head and his easel and quiver of brushes sticking out of his pack. "Mr. Honeywell!" I exclaimed. I was so glad to see him! Only then did I realize how lonely and scared I'd felt with just the empty husk of Ezra for company.

I was worried how Ezra would take to having a stranger show up so sudden. A quick glance showed him to be staring into the fire, but I could see he'd froze up, and hunkered himself down, the way wild creatures do when they hope not to be noticed.

"This here's my friend," I said. "The one I was looking for." I said it kind of slow and meaningful, hoping Honeywell might remember some of our conversation and go easy.

"Ah, yes," he said quietly. "I am glad to see you've been reunited." He stood where he was, and I was grateful to him for it.

"Ezra," I said, "this here's Joseph Honeywell. He's a portrait maker I met on the way out to find you. I'll ask him to set a spell with us, if you don't mind."

Ezra sat still and quiet, and I gestured for Honeywell

to come on over. He did, after setting his pack down. His movements were slow and deliberate as he took a seat on the side of the fire away from Ezra.

"How have you been?" I asked after a moment or two.

"Far as I know, I ain't died since you saw me last, and that's something," he said.

I laughed.

"How'd you get shed of that no-account peddler?" he asked. "Did he finally get strung up for a thief and a liar?"

"Should have, I reckon," I said darkly. "He stole my half eagle and told me you were the one did it."

To my surprise, Honeywell let out a guffaw, like that was about the funniest thing he'd heard in days.

I scowled, not getting the joke.

"I wondered how long it'd take him to relieve you of whatever it was you had hanging round your neck," Honeywell said.

I felt my mouth drop open. "You knew about it, too, then?" I asked.

"Well, sure," he said cheerfully. "I told you I ain't dead yet, and I reckon I ain't blind or stupid, either. It's a nice twist, I have to admit, him pinning it on me. When you caught him at it, I imagine he told you it was for your own good, so's you'd learn a lesson."

I shook my head in amazement. He read people like books, same as Beckwith did.

"That Beckwith's a right scoundrel," Honeywell said,

chuckling to himself all the while. I could see that, in spite of all the smart remarks and insults they traded back and forth, Honeywell was fond of Beckwith.

At first I was surprised, but then I realized I felt no real gripe with the peddler myself. He'd gotten me to Ezra, which was just what he'd said he would do. I'd got my coin back, and though I didn't like to admit it, he *had* taught me a thing or two.

"How'd you happen upon your friend here?" Honeywell asked.

I told him the story of finding Ezra in Milltown, and how we escaped from the Trasks. Honeywell was a good audience, and his admiring remarks made me feel that I'd done something awful brave.

Then he looked at Ezra and said, "I wonder about your experiences before you met up with Trask."

He didn't say it like he expected an answer, more like he was just talking to himself. Ezra stared into the fire.

"You left us a letter in the stone wall, Ezra, remember?" I asked. "It said you were going to find your wife's kinfolk."

I wasn't sure if talking about his murdered wife would bring him happy memories or sad ones, but I figured he'd feel *something*. If he did, I couldn't tell.

To Honeywell, I added, "They're Shawnees, removed by the government to the territories out west."

Honeywell nodded. "I heard about that," he said. Then he shook his head. "It wasn't a pretty story."

I glanced at Ezra. He didn't look up, but his back stiffened, and he seemed alert in a way he hadn't before.

"What did you hear?" I asked.

"Well, I ran into some traders who'd been to the territories," Honeywell began. "As they told it, the Shawnees were led out there by agents from the War Department. The idea was they'd leave early enough in the spring so's they'd get to their new home in time to start out fresh, planting and so on. But one thing and another came up to delay them. Government bungling, mostly. Supplies that were promised didn't show up or got stolen. Word was, some of the government agents were the ones did the stealing."

Honeywell lifted one eyebrow and gave me a little smile. "I hope that doesn't shock you, young Nathan."

I shook my head.

He went on. "Well, anyhow, the Shawnees were told to sell their cattle and hogs and all their property that was considered too burdensome to take with them. So they did.

"And the word got out, as it will, that they had money. All sorts of unscrupulous tradesmen showed up to sell the Injuns whiskey, with the idea that, once they were drunk, it'd be easy to fleece 'em out of their money. Which it was.

"Like I said, they'd sold their livestock, so they had no meat. The government rations of flour and meal never showed, so they were living on pumpkins and potatoes. It got to be late in the year before they actually set out, and they ran into rain and snow and real bad cold. Lots died of dysentery and other sicknesses. The ones who got there were in pretty bad shape."

Honeywell sighed, and picked up a stick to stir the fire. "Time will tell, I reckon, how they manage."

During Honeywell's telling, Ezra hadn't moved. But this was a different kind of stillness. I could tell he'd been listening.

"Were you there, Ezra?" I asked quietly. "Is that really how it happened?"

In the light from the fire I saw the track of a single tear make its way slowly down his sunken cheek.

We didn't talk anymore after that. I put my fiddle away without playing, and lay on my back thinking for a long time before I fell asleep. It *was* an ugly tale Honeywell had told, and I was sorry that Ezra's memory of it had been stirred. It had pained me to see that tear run down his face. But that tear meant Ezra could hear and understand and feel things. And that meant he was coming back from the dark place he'd gone to, didn't it?

18

I AWOKE TO HONEYWELL wrestling with his boots.

"I can never get my feet into these things till after I've had 'em on for a while," he said, giving me a toothy grin.

I laughed, and it seemed a fine way to start out the day. Ezra stirred soon after that. There was nothing I could point to that was different about the way he acted as we ate and prepared to leave. But something had changed. For the first time, he seemed mindful of the things going on around him.

It came time to part company with Honeywell, and I didn't want to say good-bye. "Where you headed?" I asked him.

"Don't know exactly," he said. "But I reckon I'm on my way there."

I said, "I wish you'd come along with us."

"I'd like that, too, Nathan," he said kindly, "but in my line of work, I have to go where there's people whose portraits need making."

"Well," I said, "you could paint me and Molly and Ezra and Pa, and then you could start in on Duffy and Winston and Job and Golly. That's our dogs and our horse and cow, and after that, there's the chickens."

We both laughed at the idea.

"Someday when a woolly-headed old coot shows up at your door, I'll remind you I was invited."

"I won't need reminding," I told him.

We said our good-byes after that. Honeywell shook my hand. Then he took a firm hold of Ezra's hand and shook it, too. I did appreciate the way he treated Ezra just the same as anybody else.

That night, after Ezra and I made camp and ate, I took out my fiddle and played as usual. I didn't think about where to place my fingers on the strings or how to hold the bow. I just played. I was feeling sorry about taking leave of Honeywell, and sad about what Ezra had seen happen to the Shawnees, and I was longing for this journey to be over so I could see Pa and Molly and the animals, too.

Eli had told me that one day I wouldn't have to think about my playing, I'd just be able to feel it. I reckon maybe that's what happened. Anyhow, I got so wrapped up in what I was doing I forgot to look at Ezra for a while.

He was sitting cross-legged, the way he always did. When I raised my eyes from the fiddle for a moment, I saw that his foot was tapping along, ever so slightly, to the music.

I looked away, so's not to make him shy, and kept playing. Every once in a while I'd take a peek, and sure enough, there was that foot movin' to the rhythm.

It's hard to describe how excited I felt. When I finally put away the fiddle and curled up in my blanket, I stared at the stars for the longest time, holding on to the hopeful feeling I'd got from seeing that tapping toe.

After that, I played my fiddle with one eye on Ezra and watched as his fingers joined his toes in tapping. Then his head began nodding to the music, too.

One evening after I finished an especially lively tune, I called out, "Whoo-ee, Ezra, what did you think of that?"

And I could have sworn the corners of his mouth turned up just the tiniest bit.

Late the next day, I began to recognize the look of the countryside and I knew we were getting close to home. I reckon my feet knew it, too, 'cause they started moving faster. Ezra had grown strong enough so he didn't have any trouble keeping up with me.

It was close to sunset when we came to a familiar ridge, and I looked down through the opening in the trees at our farm. The fields were ripe with their harvest colors. In Mama's garden, a row of sunflowers shone bright in the last rays of daylight. Golly stood in the pen by the barn, waiting to be milked and fed. Molly and Pa were in the far field, loading squash into the wagon. Pa gazed toward the setting sun, stretched his back, and seemed to say something to Molly. Then he took Job by the harness, and they started leading him back to the barn for the night. I stood, taking it all in, and my heart swelled at the sight.

Then, loud as I could, I whistled between my teeth the way Pa had showed me. The sound carried across our little valley. Pa and Molly both turned to look our way. Pa waved and held on to Job, who had shied a bit at the sudden noise. Molly's hand flew to her mouth; then she began running toward us. Duffy and Winston came from behind the barn and started after her.

The dogs reached us first, barking with excitement and jumping up to lick our hands and faces.

"Nathan! Ezra!" Molly gasped, hardly able to speak for breathing hard and smiling so big. She threw one arm around my waist and the other around Ezra's and hugged so hard I could barely breathe myself. When she finally let go, she stepped back and looked from me to Ezra, and there was no mistaking her joy in seeing us.

I dreaded the moment when she would realize that, although I'd found Ezra and brought him home with me, he wasn't really there. But I don't reckon anyone can resist my sister, Molly. When I turned to Ezra, he was looking back at her, and his lean, worn face had cracked open in a smile that reached clear to his eyes.

"Ezra!" she cried. "I knew you'd come back!"

19

I RECKON I TALKED the hind leg off a donkey all through supper and long after, too. Molly and Pa asked lots and lots of questions. For his part, Ezra listened and nodded and even smiled a bit. It was almost like before, although we could see that the effort of it tired him out.

I held back some when it came to telling about the Trasks. I didn't want Molly to know everything about them and their show and what it had been like for Ezra. I figured Ezra had lived through it and didn't need to hear it, either, far as that went.

Molly and Pa carried on about how brave I'd been to sneak Ezra out of there right under the noses of the Trasks. I said I'd never have managed it without Calvin, Pea-Head Pete, Amelia, Betty, and especially Little Miss Mary. Their mouths dropped wide open as I told them about facing Trask down that night under the moon.

Next I told about how I'd met up with Honeywell, not once, but twice. Even Ezra seemed to like hearing about how Honeywell and Beckwith carried on, joking and fooling back and forth.

"Honeywell said he might show up here someday," I said. "I hope he does, so's you can see the man for your own selves."

Molly couldn't get enough of hearing about the savage Devil-Beast of Borneo. She plain couldn't believe two men fooled a whole town that way.

"Oh, I ran into every sort of person there is," I said, feeling pretty full of myself, what with all the attention I was getting. "There's regular folks, sure. But there's also clever swindlers and scoundrels most everywhere you go. Beckwith isn't half bad, I reckon, compared to Trask. And Trask isn't even the worst sort, when you consider he could have shot me and didn't.

"You see, Molly," I said, "you got to learn to read folks, just like you read a book. I've been working on it. It's how I knew to trust Miss Mary and them, and how I knew—well, *hoped*, anyway—Trask wasn't a killer."

Molly was listening wide-eyed. Pa didn't say anything, but he nodded at that, and I could see he was pleased.

I reached around my neck and gave Molly back her locket.

"I wish I could have brought home Mama's half eagle gold piece, too," I said to Pa. I'd already told them about how Beckwith took it and how I got it back. I'd explained how I'd had to cut it to pay for the knife, and how I'd finished off the knife using it to cut through the shackles.

"I believe your mama would be mighty proud at how you put that coin to use," Pa said quietly, and that made me feel real good.

"Come spring," I told Pa, "Beckwith will most likely show up again. I was hoping you could buy yourself those spectacles."

"With the good crop we had, I believe I will," Pa answered.

"And some hair ribbons and combs for Miss Abigail," I added with a grin.

Pa's face turned red, as it always did when Miss Abigail's name was mentioned, and he said it was time we all got to bed.

The weeks passed, turning the leaves red and gold, then brown. Ezra grew strong, eating Molly's good food, and he helped us bring in the rest of the squash, beans, corn, and apples. I reckon it was his way of saying thanks for coming after him.

Slowly, though, the knowledge grew in me that he wouldn't stay with us in our cabin forever. Pa and Molly and me, we'd have liked it if he did. But it wasn't Ezra's way.

One day, when the harvest was in and the wind carried winter on its breath, Ezra disappeared into the woods and didn't come back until close to dark.

It happened again, and again, and the third time I followed him. He traveled the same way he'd gone the night he'd come and led Molly and me through the darkness to where Pa lay near to dying. When after many hours he reached his we-gi-wa, I hid and watched. I saw that he'd put new sheets of bark on the sides and the roof. He was gathering firewood and piling it near the doorway.

I knew then that he'd be leaving us soon. I turned away, not wanting him to see me or the tears that prickled my eyes, and started my long walk home.

The day came when he left and didn't come back. Molly cried and cried. I might have, too, if I hadn't seen it coming and done a lot of thinking on it.

I figured it wasn't for me, or Molly, or Pa to decide how Ezra should live. Getting him away from Trask was different. He didn't belong there, just like Little Miss Mary had said.

The hard thing was, he didn't belong with us, either. It pained me because I loved him. I believe he loved me and Molly and Pa, too, in his way. But his way was different, and I reckon a body would need to have lived his whole life inside Ezra's skin to know what it was like being him.

The world had given Ezra more than his share of sorrow, that was certain. But he'd fit the pieces of his broken heart back together once before, and I hoped he'd be able to do it again. He'd made a good start, by coming back from a place much farther away than Pennsylvania. There was still a ways to go, and I reckoned it might take him some time.

I wished I could explain it all to Molly. "Ezra's gone to

his we-gi-wa," I told her. "He's got it all fixed up again. I followed him there, the day when I was gone and didn't get back till after dark."

"But *why*?" she wailed.

"I think it's because it's where he lived with his wife," I said. "They were happy there. I reckon he's going back to try to be happy there again."

Molly sniffled, appearing to be thinking about it.

"Maybe he'll find another wife," I said, adding, "same as Pa might do."

She smiled a little bit at that.

"He's not gone for good, Molly. He'll come back to see us, I bet, and I'm sure Pa will let us visit him sometimes."

"But it's so far away," she said sadly.

I thought of something Orrin Beckwith said to Honeywell one day. It had made me grin like a roast possum at the time, and I smiled, remembering it. I hoped it would make Molly smile, too.

"It seems farther than it is, Molly," I told her. "But once you get there, you'll find it ain't."